"You may think you're fine, but you're not. If you don't want to talk about it right now, that's your decision. You have forty-three more days to talk about it. Do you have any more questions?"

All I could do was sit there for a minute or two, watching him watch me. "What do you mean I have forty-three more days?" I asked him finally.

"You're in a forty-five day program," he told me. "You've been more or less awake for two days, counting today, which leaves you with forty-three more to go."

"What kind of program?" I said.

"To determine the cause of your distress and work on your healing process," he told me like he was reading a brochure. "You'll participate in individual counseling sessions with me and in group counseling with some of the other patients."

"Other patients?" I said. "What other patients?"

"Other young people," Cat Poop told me. "You'll meet some of them tomorrow."

"Why?" I asked. "Are we having a sing-along?"

ALSO BY MICHAEL THOMAS FORD

Z

michael thomas ford

SUICIDE NOTES

A NOVEL

HARPER TEEN
An Imprint of HarperCollins*Publishers*

HarperTeen is an imprint of HarperCollins Publishers.

Suicide Notes
www.harperteen.com

Library of Congress Cataloging-in-Publication Data
Ford, Michael Thomas.
    Suicide notes / Michael Thomas Ford. — 1st ed.
        p.   cm.
    Summary: Brimming with sarcasm, fifteen-year-old Jeff describes his
stay in a psychiatric ward after attempting to commit suicide.
    ISBN 978-0-06-073757-3
    [1. Suicide—Fiction. 2. Psychiatric hospitals—Fiction. 3. Homo-
sexuality—Fiction.] I. Title.
PZ7.F7532119Su 2008   2008019199
[Fic]—dc22   CIP
                                                                 AC

Typography by Amy Ryan
15 16 17 18   LP/RRDC   10

First paperback edition, 2010

For ABBY McADEN,
WHO TOLD ME TO WRITE IT

LEXA HILLYER,
WHO MADE IT BETTER

AND SARAH SEVIER,
WHO SAW IT THROUGH

DAY 01

I read somewhere that when astronauts come back to Earth after floating around in space they get sick to their stomachs because the air here smells like rotting meat to them. The rest of us don't notice the stink because we breathe it every day and to us it smells normal, but really the air is filled with all kinds of pollutants and chemicals and junk that we put into it. Then we spray other crap around to try and make it smell better, like the whole planet is someone's old car and we've hung this big pine-scented air freshener from the rearview mirror.

I feel like those astronauts right now. For a while I was floating around in space breathing crystal-pure oxygen and talking to the Man in the Moon. Then suddenly everything changed and I was falling through the stars. I used to wonder what it would be like to be a meteor. Now I know. You fall and fall and fall, and then you're surrounded by clouds and your whole body tingles as it starts to burn up from the entry into the atmosphere. But you're falling so fast that it burns only for a second, and then the ocean comes rushing up at you and you laugh and laugh, until the water closes over your head and you're sinking. Then you know you're safe—you've survived the fall—and as you come back to the surface you blow millions of bubbles into the blue-green water.

Only then your head breaks through the waves and you suck in great breaths of stinking air and you want to die, like babies when they come out of their mothers and find out that they should have stayed inside where they were safe. That's where I am now, floating in the ocean like a piece of space junk and trying not to throw up every time I breathe.

I'm not really in the ocean, though. I'm in the hospital. They say they brought me here last night, but I was totally out of it and don't remember anything. Actually, what I heard someone say was that I was kind of dead. Pretty close to dead, anyway.

I really do think I was flying around in space, though. At least for a little while. I remember thinking that I'd finally find out whether anyone lives on Mars or not. Then it was like someone grabbed me by the foot and yanked me down, back toward Earth. I remember screaming that I didn't want to go, but since you can't make noise in space, my voice was just kind of eaten up.

Now that I know where I am, I'm not so sure I wouldn't be better off just being dead.

And maybe I *am* dead. I mean, it does kind of feel like Hell around here. I'm in this room with people checking in on me every five seconds. And by people I mean nurses, and in particular Nurse Goody. Can you believe that? Her name is actually Nurse Goody. And she is, too. Good, I mean. She's always smiling and asking me if she can get me anything. It's really annoying, because all I *want* is to be left alone, and that's the last thing they seem to do here. So many people run in and out of this room, I feel like a tourist attraction. I bet Nurse Goody is standing outside the door selling tickets, like those guys at carnivals who try to get people to pay to see the freak show. Barkers, I think they're called. That's what Nurse Goody is, a barker. She stands outside my door and barks.

But it's not like there's anything interesting in here. No television. No roommate (which actually, now that I think about it, is probably a good thing). Not even any magazines or books. Just me in bed looking out the window, which is the kind with wire running through the glass so you can't break it and jump out. The paint around the windows is all chipped, like maybe someone who was in here before me *tried* to break the window, then decided to claw their way out instead.

Now that I look at it, the whole room is kind of old-looking. The walls are this dirty white color, and there are some cracks in the plaster, and a weird brown spot on the ceiling that looks like a face. The Devil's face, maybe. Because, like I said, I think I might be in Hell. It would make sense that he would be watching me. Him and Nurse Goody are watching me. Good and Evil.

That's funny. Good and Evil. Maybe I'm not in Hell. Maybe I'm in that in-between place. What do they call it? Limbo. Where all the dead people go who don't have a "go directly to Heaven or Hell" card. Dead babies go there, too, I think. People no one knows what to do with, and dead babies. My kind of people.

Maybe I'm in Limbo, and the Devil and Goody are fighting over me. Or waiting for me to make up my mind where I want to go. What would I pick, Heaven or Hell? That's a good question. Seriously, I think I would pick Hell. The people there would probably be more interesting.

Come to think of it, it really is hot as Hell in here. There's a radiator under the window, the big old metal kind that shakes whenever water goes through it. I guess it's been working overtime. I swear, this place must be eleventy years old. It's like any minute now the whole building is going to fall apart. At least then I wouldn't be here.

It's raining, and the only thing I can see out the window is part of a forest. Since it's winter, though, it looks less like a forest and more like a bunch of skeletons holding their hands up to the sky. The rain is running down the glass, making it look like the skeletons are under water. Drowning. Although if they're skeletons, wouldn't they already be dead? So maybe they're just swimming. Anyway, the skeleton trees are kind of freaking me out. It's looking more and more like this really is Hell. Maybe I should tell Goody she's in the wrong place.

I'm really tired. The radiator is rattling, it's hot in

here, and my head hurts. I keep looking up at the Devil's face, and I think he's laughing at me. I sort of wish Goody would come in and make him shut up. Maybe she's given up on me.

I know they're hoping I'll say something about why I did what I did. So for the record: I just felt like it.

Day 02

This just gets better and better.

It turns out I really *am* in the hospital. Not Limbo. I'm pretty sure that it *is* Hell. Because I'm not just in the hospital. I'm in the mental ward. You know, where they keep the people who have sixteen imaginary friends living in their heads and can't stop picking invisible bugs off their bodies. Whackos. Nut-jobs. Total losers.

I'm not crazy. I don't see what the big deal is about what happened. But apparently someone *does* think it's a big deal because here I am. I bet it was my mother. She always overreacts.

They weren't going to tell me—you know, about

the mental ward thing—but I found out when Goody left my chart next to the bed while she went to get something at the desk. Someone should tell her that you really shouldn't leave something like that lying around if you don't want someone to look at it.

Anyway, I just happened to pick up the chart, because that's what I do when someone leaves something around and I want to know what it is, and right there on the top of the first page it said PSYCHIATRIC WARD. At first I figured it was someone else's file, but then I saw my name. Let me tell you something, seeing your name and PSYCHIATRIC WARD on the same piece of paper isn't the best way to start your day.

When Goody came back she saw me looking at the file and the smile plastered to her face finally disappeared. "You're not supposed to be looking at that," she said, like I didn't know and would apologize.

"This is a psych ward?" I said, trying to read as much as I could before she grabbed the folder, which she did about two seconds later.

"It's time for your medication," she said.

"Uh-uh," I told her. "Not until someone tells me why I'm here."

"I think you know why you're here," she said, giving me that look people give you when they know *you* know what they mean.

"I'm not crazy," I said.

"Nobody said you were crazy," said Goody, her smile returning. Suddenly she was all happy again, like there'd been a momentary blackout in her reception and now we'd returned to the regularly scheduled program.

"That file does," I shot back. "It says it in big letters."

"Take your pill," she said, ignoring me. "You'll feel better."

"No," I told her. "I don't even know what it is."

Goody smiled, which was starting to get on my nerves. "It's a sedative," she said.

"So you're drugging me?" I said. "Why? What the hell is going on here?"

Goody took the paper cup she was holding out to me and put it back on the tray by my bed. "I think maybe you should talk to Dr. Katzrupus."

"Catwhatsis?" I asked her. "Cat Poopus? What kind of name is that?"

"Katzrupus," she said again. "I'll get him."

She disappeared, taking my file with her, which she totally should have done the first time, because then we wouldn't have had this problem. At least not right now. After she left, I stared at the cup with the pill in it. It was a small red pill, round like a ladybug. I almost took it, just to see what it would do, but I didn't want Goody to think I thought I needed it or anything, which I don't.

Goody came back a minute later with some guy. He was short, with really wild black hair that was about three weeks past needing to be cut, and he looked like he hadn't shaved in a couple of days either. He seemed way too young to be a doctor, and at first I thought he was some kind of student doctor or something, like I didn't even rate a real one.

"I'm Dr. Katzrupus," he said, holding out his hand.

"Why am I in the nuthouse?" I asked him, staring at his hand without shaking it.

"You're not in a nuthouse," he said, taking his hand back and pushing his glasses up his nose. "You're in a hospital."

"Right," I said. "The nut ward in a hospital."

"It's a *psychiatric* ward," he said. "And you're in it because we're concerned that something might be bothering you." He spoke in this really calm and casual way, as if he was telling you what he had for dinner. For some reason, that really bugged me.

"Something might be bothering me," I repeated,

mimicking his voice. Then I laughed. "Why would something be bothering me?"

Cat Poop got this weird look on his face, like he didn't know what to say. I just kept staring at him.

"Are my parents around here somewhere?" I asked. "'Cause if they are, I'd really like to go home now."

"We need to run a few tests," he said. "And, no, your parents aren't here."

I thought it was kind of weird that my parents weren't there, and I wanted to ask where they were instead of being with their kid in the hospital, but I didn't. "I'm not so good at tests," I said instead. "Especially pop quizzes. Could I maybe have some study time first? I wouldn't want to bring the curve down for the whole class or anything."

He looked at me for a second. Then he said, "I'll see you later this afternoon."

After he left Goody came back with this other guy who I swear to God was a vampire. He took what seemed like three gallons of blood out of me, test tube after test tube of it. After the fourth one I started to feel really sick.

Finally, the Human Leech and Goody went away with his tray of tubes and a woman came in. "I'm Miss

Pinch," she said. I swear. I'm not making it up. I don't know what it is with the names around here. I'm not sure this isn't all a dream, because in the real world people just aren't named things like Nurse Goody and Miss Pinch and Dr. Cat Poop.

"I need to ask you a few questions," Miss Pinch told me, pulling a chair up beside my bed.

Turns out that was the understatement of the year, unless to you "a few" means eight thousand and sixty-two.

"Have you ever taken Ecstasy?" Miss Pinch asked me, smiling and cocking her head like a bird. An irritating, nosy little bird.

"No," I told her, and she made a check mark on the folder she was holding.

"Methamphetamine?" she said. When I didn't answer right away she added, "Crystal? Ice? Tina?"

"I know what it is," I told her. "And no, I've never taken it."

She made another mark. And she kept making marks after every question and answer. Cocaine? No. Check. Alcohol? No. Check. Marijuana, GHB, snappers? No, no, no. Check, check, check.

I kept answering no to everything, because I really haven't ever done drugs, and she kept looking at me like maybe I was lying just to get her out of there. So finally I said that yes, okay, I'd smoked pot a few times, and that seemed to make her happy. Like it's not possible that there's a kid on this planet who hasn't smoked pot. Moron.

"How about glue?" she asked me.

I nodded, and she lit up like a Christmas tree. At least until I said, "I used to eat paste. In kindergarten. Bad habit. I totally gave it up, though. I swear. It didn't mix with the apple juice so well."

I have to say, I was a little disappointed that she wasn't madder than she was. Maybe talking to crazy people all the time makes you kind of immune to it. She just kept asking and checking. After we went through every drug known to science, Pinch said, "Now let's talk about sexual activity."

"Let's not," I said, giving her the same big smile she was giving me.

"Have you ever—" she started to say.

"Seriously," I said, interrupting her. "Let's not. It's none of your damn business."

"I'm only trying to help you," she said, still smiling.

"Well, you're not," I informed her. "You're just pissing me off. Now go away."

She stared at me.

"Seriously," I said. "Get out of here. There's nothing wrong with me. I answered your stupid questions about the drugs, and I'm not telling you anything else because there's nothing else you need to know. So either go away or else sit there while I take a nap, because this is the last thing I'm saying to you."

She snapped her file shut and stood up. "I'll just get the doctor," she said.

That seems to be what they do around here when you say no to them, like the doctors are the National Guard or something. So once again I got a visit from good old Cat Poop. This time he shut the door so that we were alone. I pictured Goody Two-shoes and Pinchface standing outside, pressing their ears to the door to try and hear what the doctor was saying.

"You're not making this very easy," he said.

"Sorry," I said. "I guess my kindergarten teacher was right when she said I don't play well with others."

"We want to help you."

"You know, everyone keeps saying that," I told him. "But I have to tell you, I'm starting to think you don't. Because if you did, you'd let me out of here. There's nothing wrong with me."

"There's evidence to the contrary," said Cat Poop.

"I'm fine," I said. "Really. Do you want me to sign

something saying that? Then will you let me go home?"

"I'm afraid that's not an option," he said.

"What about my parents?" I asked him. "Where are they? Tell them I want to go home now."

"Your parents agree that you need to spend some time here," he answered.

"You can't keep me here against my will," I informed him. "In case you don't know, this is the land of the *free*. People have rights. I have the right to free speech, and to bear arms, and to not be locked up in a nuthouse!" I knew what I was talking about. I mean, I've read the Constitution. In sixth grade, and I don't remember exactly what it said. But still.

Cat Poop looked at me for a moment, then said really calmly, "You're in a psychiatric ward because you attempted to commit suicide. You may think you're fine, but you're not. If you don't want to talk about it right now, that's your decision. You have forty-three more days to talk about it. Do you have any more questions?"

All I could do was sit there for a minute or two, watching him watch me. "What do you mean I have forty-three more days?" I asked him finally.

"You're in a forty-five-day program," he told me.

"You've been more or less awake for two days, counting today, which leaves you with forty-three more to go."

"What kind of program?" I said.

"To determine the cause of your distress and work on your healing process," he told me like he was reading a brochure. "You'll participate in individual counseling sessions with me and in group counseling with some of the other patients."

"Other patients?" I said. "What other patients?"

"Other young people," Cat Poop told me. "You'll meet some of them tomorrow."

"Why?" I asked. "Are we having a sing-along?"

"If you want to," he said. "But usually the patients just sit in a circle and look at each other until someone decides to talk."

"I don't have anything to talk about," I informed him.

"Then you have forty-three days of staring to look forward to," he said. "Is there anything else you'd like to discuss?"

"How about the environment?" I suggested. "Maybe the effects of greenhouse gases on the Amazon rain forests? Or what will happen when the polar ice cap melts? Did you know all the polar bears are drowning because they have nothing to sit on?"

"Perhaps another time," he said. "I have rounds to make. We'll hold off on the rest of your evaluation until you're in a more cooperative mood."

"Good luck with that one," I called after him as he left.

He's wrong about the suicide thing, by the way. This is just a big misunderstanding. I'll sort it out in the next couple of days and then I'll be out of here. In the meantime, maybe I *will* take the ladybug pill. If I have to be here, I might as well get in a good nap. And, really, I kind of like how these pills make me feel. I'll have to remember to tell Pinch. She'll get a kick out of it.

Day 03

There are five of us. In the fun house, I mean. Well, five kids. There are a bunch of adult whack-jobs, too, but they have their own ward. We get our very own Baby Nuthouse all to ourselves. It's just like at Thanksgiving, when all the kids get sent to the little table in the corner. No turkey legs for us. Just the parts no one else wants. Like giblets.

Let me clarify. There are four of *them* and one of me. I met the others today in my first group therapy session. I wasn't going to go, but I figured if I show everyone how completely sane I am, they'll have to let me out. The group sessions are held in what they call the community room, which is just this big room with couches and a TV and games and stuff. I guess it's where all the crazies hang out when they're not busy being crazy.

We sat in a circle on these hard plastic chairs. They're orange—traffic-cone orange—like they're a warning to anyone who might walk in. DANGER: CRAZY PEOPLE TALKING. TAKE ALTERNATE ROUTE. Besides being ugly, they're also really unpleasant to sit on. After about five minutes my butt fell asleep, and I kept having to move around to try and get comfortable. Which I never did.

Cat Poop introduced me by saying, "Everyone, this is Jeff." And they all went, "Hi, Jeff." Only their voices all sounded the same, like zombies mumbling, "Mmmm, brains," and nobody really looked at me. I didn't say anything. It's not like I'm going to be here long enough to make friends.

After that we sat in a circle just staring at each other, just like Cat Poop said we would. Nobody said a word until finally the doc pointed at this skinny girl with long blonde hair who was chewing at her finger-nails and said, "Alice, why don't you tell Jeff a little bit about yourself."

"My name is Alice," said the girl. Duh. "What should you know about me? Well, my mother's latest boyfriend kept coming into my bedroom when I was asleep and putting himself all over me, so one night I waited until *he* was sleeping and I went into his room with some lighter fluid and matches. He didn't die or anything, but I got a little burnt."

At first I thought she was making it all up. But then she held up her arms so I could see. The skin was red and raw from her hands to her elbows. Alice laughed. Then she bent her head and covered her face with her long hair.

I'm not sure if she's for real or not. My guess is that she just burnt her arms playing with matches or something stupid like that. I bet she made up the thing about torching her mother's boyfriend. I mean, that's a lot more interesting, and I wouldn't blame her for going with it. If I did something dumb like set myself on fire, I'd lie about it too.

The thing is, I don't think she did. I don't know why, but I believe her. What's even weirder is that it doesn't freak me out. I can totally see why she would set that guy on fire, which maybe makes me as crazy as she is. Then again, I didn't *do* it; I can just *imagine* doing it. Maybe that's the difference between crazy and not crazy.

Alice didn't say anything else, so we moved on to

the girl beside her. She was almost the exact opposite of Alice: fat, curly red hair, a face like the moon. When she saw me looking at her, she actually smiled, like we were on a bus and not in a hospital.

"My name's Juliet," she said, all happy and chirpy like a cartoon bird. "I'm Bone's girlfriend."

She paused, like I was supposed to know who Bone was, like he was some rapper or actor or something whose name was all over the magazines and I was going to congratulate her on having a famous boyfriend. When I didn't say anything Juliet nodded at the guy sitting beside me. The whole time people had been talking, he'd been looking at his feet. He barely looked up now.

"That's Bone," said Juliet, beaming like she was showing me her new car. "We're in a band. Gratuitous Sex and Violence?" she added, as if she wasn't sure herself. "Bone plays guitar. I sing."

Next to me, Bone sighed and crossed his arms over his chest. He was wearing a white T-shirt, and he had lots of tattoos, even though I don't think he's a whole lot older than I am. My parents would never let me get a tattoo, so it's kind of impressive that he has so many. I looked at them for a second, but none of them were really interesting. Just lots of flaming skulls and naked girls on motorcycles and stuff like that. He had hair he obviously dyed because it was too black to be natural, and eyes that didn't seem to focus on anything. His eyes were black, too, like his hair. He looked like a comic book drawing.

"Which one of you is sex and which one of you is violence?" I asked.

"What?" Juliet asked, her smile slipping.

"Gratuitous sex and violence," I said slowly, as if I was talking to a really little kid. "Which of you is which?"

Juliet looked at Bone, like he was going to give her the answer. He just kept staring at his feet. Juliet ran a hand over her mouth as if she was trying to wipe something away that wasn't there. Someone else started to laugh, but stopped.

"Um, it's not really . . . ," she said, sounding confused. "It's just a, you know, a name."

"She's not my girlfriend," Bone said suddenly, looking up for a second. "She just thinks she is. There is no band. I don't even know her, okay?"

Juliet looked at him and started to say something, but Cat Poop spoke before she could. "Why don't we move on," he said. He reminded me of a tour guide at one of those historic places where they take you

22

through in little groups to make sure you don't touch the eight-million-year-old candlesticks or whatever. "Why don't we move on" isn't really a question, because you don't have a choice; it's just a passive-aggressive way of saying, "Get the hell out of here. There's another bunch of tourists who want to see the candlesticks."

So Cat Poop made us leave the bedroom where Abraham Lincoln freed the slaves and go to the kitchen where they were baking bread just like they did two hundred years ago. Actually, he just nodded at the next person, a girl sitting beside Juliet.

"Okay," she said. "My name is Sadie. I'm a Libra, I like sunny days and kittens, and think pollution and negative people are real downers. Oh, and I tried to drown myself and this guy saved me and so I'm not dead."

She looked right at me, like she was daring me to ask a question. Her eyes were this really intense blue, like the ice at the North Pole. She had black hair, cut short and spiky, and pale skin, which made her eyes look even bluer. The best way to describe her is to say she looked like an evil pixie, or at least a troublemaking one.

Bone was next, but all he did was say "I'm Bone" and go back to his feet. I was hoping he'd say more about the girl who wasn't his girlfriend, or what it was like being a walking cartoon, but I guess he thought he'd told us enough already.

So then it was my turn. I really didn't want to say anything, but Bone had already done the silent and mysterious thing, and I knew if I did it too I would look like I was trying to be like him.

"I'm Jeff," I said. "I'm here because they think I need to be. But I don't. There's not much else to tell."

"What's with the bandages, then?"

Sadie was nodding at my lap. I looked down and saw that the cuffs of my shirt had ridden up, and some gauze was sticking out of the bottom.

"Nothing," I said. "Just a cut."

"Okay," said Cat Poop. "Now that Jeff knows a little more about you, today I want to talk about what it means to tell the truth."

That's when I zoned out. Actually, I just kind of settled into this warm, foggy place where everything faded out and voices sounded like planes flying somewhere way faraway. I knew people were talking, but I wasn't listening. I wasn't interested in anything anyone had to say. I mean, telling the truth? What a lame thing to talk about. The *truth* is that I don't belong here.

Eventually the airplane noises stopped, and I

realized that group was over. Everyone was standing up. Cat Poop came over to me. "You didn't contribute much today," he said.

"Sorry," I said. "I have a lot on my mind."

"Like?" he asked.

I shrugged. "Like whether the whole boy-band craze is really over," I said. "I know people say it is, but I think they're wrong."

"Why don't I show you around," said Cat Poop. "This is the lounge. You're allowed in here as long as there's a staff member present. There are usually four people here during the day, two nurses and two order-lies, and we always have at least two nurses and a security person on at night."

"Security," I said. "Sounds serious. Is that to keep the Gratuitous Sex and Violence fans out?"

"Meals are also served in here," he continued, ignoring me and pointing to two long tables sur-rounded by more plastic chairs. "You've been allowed to eat in your room, but from now on you'll eat with the rest of the floor. Food is brought up from the hos-pital cafeteria."

"Just like one big happy family," I remarked as we left the lounge and walked down the hallway toward my room.

"You each have your own room," Cat Poop said. "Boys on this end, girls on the other. You may not be in another person's room unsupervised. There are bathrooms on either end of the hall."

"Can we be in *there* with each other unsupervised?" I asked. "Or is peeing at the same time frowned upon?"

"You'll be given a schedule for each day," he went on. "You'll be keeping up with your schoolwork while you're here. We'll see about getting your books and assignments from your school."

"You're telling the people at my school that I'm here?" I said. I was already imagining Principal Matthews giving the morning announcement. "*Today's lunch will be spaghetti and meatballs, cheerleading tryouts will be held second period in the gym, and Jeff is in the nuthouse.*"

"They'll be told that you're going to be out for some time," Cat Poop said. "That's all."

"Great," I said. "And here I thought I'd found the perfect way to get out of that algebra test."

"As I told you earlier," Cat Poop continued, "you'll participate in group sessions, as well as individual sessions with me."

"Are those supervised too?" I asked him. "I mean,

what if you try to, you know, touch me inappropriately or something?"

Cat Poop stopped and turned to me. He handed me a sheet of paper. "Here's your schedule for today. You have some free time now. I suggest you spend it getting to know the other people here."

"Sure," I told him as I folded up my schedule without looking at it. "They seem like swell kids."

"Give them a chance," he said. "You might be surprised."

"I'll take your word on that," I said. "You know, if this whole shrink thing doesn't work out, you should look into getting a job at Disneyland. You're good at this guide thing. You'd rock the safari ride."

"I'll see you later this afternoon for our session," he said, without missing a beat. "My office is at the end of the other hallway off the lounge. One of the nurses will bring you down there."

After he was gone, I unfolded the schedule and looked at it. My therapy session was scheduled for three thirty. I looked at the clock on the wall. It was only twelve thirty, which meant I had three hours to kill before the Amazing Cat Poop tried to open up my head and see what was inside. Three hours to spend doing nothing.

"I have arts and crafts at one o' clock."

I looked up and saw Sadie standing by me. She waved her sheet. "Maybe I can make my dad that wallet he's always wanted."

"I was kind of hoping for archery," I told her. "But I think I'm stuck with nature trail and capture the flag."

She laughed. "Welcome to Camp Meds," she said. "Where the campers are crazy and the counselors *want* you to take drugs."

"Yeah, well, this camper isn't sticking around long," I told her, crumpling up my schedule.

"How's that?" she said. "You have a plan or something?"

"Sure," I said, throwing the ball of paper into a trash can. "And it's really simple—I'm not crazy."

Sadie laughed again. "Right," she said. "None of us are."

"I'm serious," I said.

"So am I," she told me. "You think I'm nuts?"

"You're here, aren't you?"

She nodded. "And so are you. You think you're the only mistake they've made?"

I looked at her face. She seemed totally serious.

Then I remembered what she'd said in group about trying to drown herself. She was crazy all right, and the last thing I needed was more crazy.

"I've got to go to the bathroom," I said. "I'll see you later."

Day 04

Here are the basic facts. My name is Jeff. I'm fifteen. I have a sister named Amanda who's thirteen, my parents are still married to each other, and all four of us live in a perfectly nice house in a perfectly nice neighborhood in a perfectly nice city that's exactly like a billion other cities. My parents have never beaten us, I've never been molested by a priest, I don't hate the other kids at my school any more than is normal for a kid my age, I don't listen to death metal, have an obsession with violent video games, or cut the heads off small animals for fun.

That's pretty much everything I told Cat Poop in our session today, which is a lot more than I told him yesterday, when I basically sat silent in the chair across from him until he told me I could go. Today, though, he tapped his pencil against the pad of paper he was holding and just stared at me. Apparently that's what therapists do to get you to open up. The thing is, it works. The longer he stared at me, the more I wanted to talk, if only to make him stop tapping.

I didn't want to talk about me, though, so I talked about everyone else in the group and how weird they were. This was after our second group session, in which I learned that Alice chews her hair, Juliet still loves Bone, and Bone still loves his shoes. Very deep stuff.

"I don't belong here," I informed Cat Poop, thinking maybe this just hadn't occurred to him. "These people are seriously demented. It's not good for me to be around them. I might catch something."

He didn't answer me for a minute. He just kept tapping—tap, tap, tap, tap, tap—until finally I told him if he didn't stop I was going to grab the pencil and stab myself in the throat. Then he put the pencil in his pocket.

"Why don't you think you belong here?" he asked.

"Why do you think I *do*?" I said.

He started with the staring thing again but didn't answer me. It's amazing how that guy can go forever

31

without blinking. I tried not to blink either, but my eyes got really dry. Finally I started talking again.

"Are you a real doctor?" I asked him. "I mean, with a diploma and everything?"

"I'm a psychiatrist," he said.

"So you're not really a doctor," I said.

"A psychiatrist is also a medical doctor," he told me. "A psychologist isn't."

"So what you're saying is that you think you're better than a psychologist," I said. "That's not very nice. I mean, I bet they worked hard too."

"They're two very different things," he said.

"Where did you go to school?" I asked. "A real college or one of those schools in the Caribbean?" I heard somewhere that people who can't get into real medical schools all go to the Caribbean, where apparently all you have to do is drink fruity drinks and sit on the beach for four years and they give you a diploma.

"I did my undergraduate work at the University of Chicago and got my doctorate at the University of Toronto."

"Canada," I said. "So you *did* have to go to a foreign country." I shook my head like this was a big disappointment. "I'm sorry, doc, I'm just not comfortable with your credentials. I think I need a second opinion."

"I've been working with young people for ten years," Cat Poop said. "I assure you that I'm quite qualified to help you."

"Ten years?" I said. I was kind of surprised. I didn't think he was that old. "What'd you do, start college when you were nine? Or by 'working with young people,' do you mean you were a camp counselor or something?"

I thought maybe he'd tell me how old he is, but he went back to staring. I looked around the office, ignoring him. Besides his desk, there's a couch and another chair besides the one I was sitting in. And they're not the plastic kind we have in the lounge; they're real leather ones that don't make your butt hurt. There's a bookcase with a bunch of boring-looking books in it, and a plant with pink flowers on top of it. On one of the walls there's a painting of a black-and-white dog holding a dead bird in its mouth.

He also has a window, and it doesn't have wire in it. I guess they're not afraid the shrinks will jump out. I thought about trying it, but we're on the fourth floor, and I'm pretty sure I'd break my leg if I did. Then I'd be crazy *and* in a cast, which is kind of overdoing it a little.

"I'm not like them," I said when I got tired of

looking at his office.

"Not like who?" he asked, as if he'd already forgotten what we were talking about.

"Them," I said, waving my hands around. "The rest of the group. I mean, seriously, look at them. They're crazy."

"Why do you say that?"

I held up one finger. "One tried to barbeque a guy," I said. I kept going, holding up another finger for each person I ticked off. "One is in love with another one who doesn't seem to know who she is or where he is, and one," I concluded, pointing a final finger in the air, "threw herself into a lake for no reason."

"And you feel that you're different from them?" he said.

"Um, yeah," I told him. "Don't you?"

"Tell me about your family," he said.

Like I said, my family is totally normal. Well, as normal as most families are, which means that sometimes we fight about stuff but the rest of the time we get along. We're so boring that I almost wanted to make up a bunch of drama to tell Cat Poop, like that my mother locks my sister and me in the cellar when we complain about what she made for dinner, or that my father pressures me to be the best at everything.

But my dad always says he was never good at math either, and that my As in English more than make up for my Cs in trigonometry. And my mom usually picks up dinner at China Dragon or South of the Border because when she tries to cook the stove catches on fire, so dinner at our house is never a problem.

"They're great," is what I said to Cat Poop. "Everything is totally great."

"Then why did you try to kill yourself?"

The guy has a one-track mind, and it's getting on my nerves. I waited a long time, to make him think I was seriously considering the question. Then I sighed. "Okay," I said. "I guess I can tell you."

Cat Poop straightened up a little in his chair. He took the pencil out again and held it over the pad, like he had to be ready to write down every single word of a historic speech or something.

"I did it because . . ." I hesitated, blinking and sniffing a little, like I might start to cry at any second. "I did it because . . . because I couldn't stand to live in the same world as Paris Hilton."

I waited for him to yell at me, but he just sat in his chair, scribbling on the pad. After a minute he looked up at me. "Somehow, I doubt Ms. Hilton is responsible for your troubles. As annoying as she may be, she has not, as far as I know, been responsible for any deaths. So why don't you just tell me the real reason?"

"There is no reason," I said. I was getting angry because he wasn't listening to me. "I just did it. I'm a teenager. We get bored and do stupid stuff. Now I'm over it and I want to go home."

He looked at his watch and said we were done for the day. I just wanted to get out of there, so when he told me they were taking me off one of my drugs and that I might feel a little out of it tonight I just nodded and walked out without looking at him.

Sure enough, when Goody gave me my afternoon paper cup of happy tablets, one of the blue ones was gone. For a couple of hours I was okay. Then I started feeling a little tired, and now I feel like someone kicked me in the head a few thousand times.

It's a really crappy feeling to realize that your entire outlook on your life can be controlled by some little pill that looks like a Pez, and that some weird combination of drugs can make your brain think it's on a holiday somewhere really sweet when actually you're standing naked in the middle of the school cafeteria while everyone takes pictures of you. Metaphorically. Or whatever.

DAY 05

I woke up in the middle of the night feeling like crap. I'd been having one of those bad dreams that seem to go on and on but where nothing really happens. In mine I was running through this big house being chased by something. I kept going up staircases and down hallways, looking for a way out. The whole time, whatever was chasing me was close enough that I could hear it breathing, but far enough away that I couldn't see what it was.

The house seemed to be nothing *but* hallways and stairs. No rooms. There was nowhere to hide. All I could do was keep running. Finally, I ran up a narrow staircase and came to a door. The Chasing Thing was right behind me, scratching at the stairs as it climbed. Its breathing got louder and louder, and all I wanted to do was get away from it before I saw its face. But the doorknob kept turning in my hand, going around and around and around.

Then something clicked in the lock, and I pulled the door open. I ran inside, but there was no room there. There was just blackness. And then I fell. It was like the floor just melted, and I was falling so fast that I couldn't even scream. Everything was black and cold, and the wind was shrieking in my head.

Then I woke up and I was staring at the Devil's face grinning down at me from the ceiling.

I tried to go back to sleep, but my mind was racing racing racing. Only I wasn't really thinking about anything specific. It was just this stream of words and half thoughts, like there were a thousand different channels in my brain and someone was flipping through them one after the next. I kept thinking about nothing until I was sure that if I stayed in my room for another minute I really *would* go crazy. So I got up and went into the common room. One of the night nurses, whose name I think is Nurse Moon (okay, maybe it's not, but I don't know her real name) was sitting at the desk that's against the wall that faces the hallway. She was doing a crossword puzzle.

"Do you need something?" she asked me. She sounded irritated, like I'd interrupted her attempt to figure out 32 Down.

I shook my head. "I just want to sit," I told her.

She nodded at the couch. I hadn't noticed when I came in, but Sadie was already curled up on it, watching something on television. The light flickered on her face, but no sound was coming out of the TV. She's such a freak.

When Sadie saw me, she patted the couch beside her. "Sit," she said.

I sat down next to her, not because she told me to, but because I didn't want to go back to my room. She was watching some black-and-white movie where a woman and a man were standing in an old-fashioned living room. The woman seemed upset, and the man was trying not to look at her.

"What do you mean you're leaving, Reginald?" Sadie said in a sad little voice.

I looked at her, wondering what she was talking about. She stared straight ahead.

"I told you, Daphne, I'm going to Peru to search for the lost city of Quezelacutan," she said, her voice suddenly low and angry.

I turned back to the screen, and realized that she was making up dialogue for the movie. As the woman threw herself at the man and grabbed his arm Sadie said, "Take me with you!" She made sobbing sounds. I couldn't help but laugh a little.

"Shh," said Sadie. "This is a drama. You can't laugh."

"Sorry," I said.

"You be Reginald," said Sadie.

"That's okay," I said. "This is your show."

"Don't be a jerk," said Sadie. "Just do it."

I didn't feel like arguing, so I played along. In the film, the man was trying to pry the woman off him. "I can't take you to Peru, Daphne," I said quickly, trying to think. "There's no room on the boat."

"But I'm small," Sadie said. "And I don't eat much. Look how skinny I am."

"No, Daphne," I answered. "Peru is no place for a woman, even a skinny one. You'll get malaria and die."

"But I speak Peruvian!" Sadie exclaimed. "I learned it at Miss Piffingham's School for Girls."

Reginald conveniently looked excited. "Why didn't you ever tell me?" I said.

"There's a lot about me you don't know, Reginald," said Sadie as the woman in the movie let go of the man and put her hands on her hips.

The movie went to a commercial. Sadie looked at me and grinned. I shook my head. "You're really nuts," I said.

"It's fun, isn't it?" Sadie said. "I do it all the time. Usually my stories are better than the real ones. At least I think so. I never actually listen to the real ones. But I'm pretty sure mine are better." She looked back at the TV. "Couldn't sleep, huh?"

I nodded. "It feels like there are twenty-three people living in my head," I told her.

"Only twenty-three?" Sadie said. "Lucky you." She looked over at Nurse Moon, then leaned toward me. "They took you off the Wonder Drug," she whispered.

"The what?"

"The Wonder Drug. It's what they put you on when you come in, so that you don't freak out or try to hurt yourself. Once they're pretty sure you won't, they take you off it. You must have been a good boy. I was on it for a whole week."

"I wish I was still on it," I said. "This sucks."

"This is the part where they try to make you remember," said Sadie. She looked at my wrists. "Is it working?"

Without realizing it, I'd pushed one sleeve of my

pajamas up and was rubbing the gauze that circled my wrist. I stopped, and let the sleeve fall back where it was.

"It will go away," Sadie told me, turning back to the television. "The stuff in your head. Little by little."

I didn't respond. I just sat and watched the television. "Do you remember?" I asked after a while.

Sadie nodded. "I wanted to float away," she said, her voice sounding all dreamy. "I was sure I could breathe underwater if I tried hard enough. Like a mermaid."

"But did you really want to die?" I asked.

She laughed. "Maybe. Maybe not. It didn't matter. And then he jumped in and saved me, anyway." She looked at me with her blue eyes. "Who saved you?"

I shrugged. "The paramedics, I guess."

Sadie shook her head. "No, they just did the work. Someone else had to save you first. Who called them?"

"My parents," I said.

"Then that's who saved you," said Sadie.

I hadn't thought about it like that. But she was right. Only was it really saving? Wasn't it more like butting in? I was thinking about this when Sadie said, "So, why *did* you do it?"

I shrugged. Even though we'd shared a little

42

moment playing the movie game, I didn't want to talk too much. Besides, there wasn't really anything to say.

"It's okay," she said. "You don't have to tell me. Let's just watch TV."

And that's what we did, with the sound off and not talking. After a while I realized that I was really tired. I said good night to Sadie and went back to my own room.

I've been thinking about Sadie, though, and how she maybe tried to drown herself. And here's what I'm wondering: How come someone always saves the people who try to kill themselves and then makes them tell everyone how sorry they are for ruining their evenings? I keep feeling like everyone wants me to apologize for something. But I'm not going to. I don't have anything to apologize for. They're the ones who screwed everything up. Not me.

I didn't ask to be saved.

DAY O6

When I was in seventh grade I had a pen pal as part of our social studies class. I guess the idea was that if we got to know kids in other parts of the world, we'd see that we're all the same and none of us would want to bomb each other when we grew up to be the presidents of our countries. Anyway, I got this girl who was part of a Masai tribe in Kenya. I didn't even know they got mail out there. I wrote her this letter about how I liked to skateboard and paint and listen to Thieving Magpies and Fun While It Lasted. She wrote me back saying her family lived in a mud hut, raised cows, and drank their blood mixed with milk, and that on Sundays they walked fifteen miles to a village to watch

Buffy the Vampire Slayer and *E.R.* on someone's TV. That's how she learned English.

She sent me a picture of herself with her body all covered in red mud, and asked me if everyone in America had swimming pools and blonde hair. I remember thinking the stamps on her letters were the most beautiful things I'd ever seen, and I made up a lot of stuff about myself because I thought she was so interesting and I was so boring. I told her my father was a famous explorer and that we went to Broadway plays all the time because my mother was in them. We wrote to each other for almost the whole school year. I forget which of us didn't answer back first. Probably me. I think I ran out of lies to tell her.

I was thinking about that today during my session with Cat Poop. Because basically he was trying to get me to tell him stuff about myself and I was making up a bunch of lies. I turned it into kind of a game. The Lying Game.

"You've been here almost a week," he said. "How are you feeling about it?"

"Oh," I said. "I really like it."

He pushed his glasses up his nose, which I realize now is something he does when he gets either nervous or excited. "You do?" he asked.

45

I nodded. "Absolutely. It's totally a four-star place you've got here. I'd knock it up to five stars, but the pool is a little cool for my liking and the room service was kind of slow bringing me my club sandwich. Not that I'm complaining. I just thought you should know."

Cat Poop set his notepad down. "Jeff," he said. "The only way this is going to work is if you start talking to me."

"I *am* talking," I reminded him. "See my mouth moving and the words coming out? That's called talking."

"You're a smart young man," he said. "It's too bad you can't turn some of that intelligence on yourself."

I knew what he was getting at. He was using that reverse-psychology thing, trying to get me to do something by saying he didn't think I *could* do it. It's totally Psych 101, and I couldn't believe he thought I would go for it. So I decided to have some real fun.

"You're right," I said, trying to sound like I meant it, which was harder than you might think. "I guess I'm just scared."

Cat Poop picked up the notebook again. His finger went right for his glasses, and I could tell he thought we were having a breakthrough. "What are you scared of?" he asked me.

I sighed really deeply, like it was totally hard for me to let my feelings out. "Everything," I told him. "I'm scared of everything."

That really got him going. His pencil flew across the paper, and he was nodding like crazy. "What are you most afraid of?" he said.

"I guess being alone," I said. "You know, having no one understand me."

He looked up. "You think no one understands you?"

"People *think* they do," I said, "but they don't. There's this whole different me in here, and nobody sees it." I touched my chest and kind of sighed.

The look on his face was priceless. I wish I'd had a camera. He totally bought the whole thing. He didn't know I was basically acting out a scene from a made-for-TV movie I'd seen once. Although in fairness to me, I *was* putting in some of my own stuff. I mean, I didn't totally rip off *The Problem with Nicole*.

"Who's inside you, Jeff?" Cat Poop asked.

I waited a while before I answered him. I wanted him to think I was revealing some big secret that only he knew. Then I leaned forward. "A ballerina," I whispered.

"I'm sorry," Cat Poop said. "A what?"

"A ballerina," I said, a little bit louder. "There's a ballerina inside of me."

He sat back in his chair and looked at me. I started talking really fast. "Yeah, see, when I was five or six, my parents took me to see *The Nutcracker*. It was the most beautiful thing I've ever seen."

I closed my eyes, like I was remembering being at the ballet. I even smiled a little. "The woman playing the Sugar Plum Fairy was wearing this pretty costume," I said. "I couldn't stop watching her. I wanted to be her."

I opened my eyes and looked at Cat Poop. "Later, I told my parents that I wanted to be the Sugar Plum Fairy. They just laughed. But it's true. I want to be her."

I leaned forward again. "She's trapped inside me," I said, really softly like maybe she might be listening and would be mad that I was talking about her. "She wants to come out."

Good old Cat Poop tapped his pencil against the pad. "You're telling me that you hurt yourself because you want to be a ballerina," he said. "Is that right?"

"Yes," I said. "It's all her fault. She made me do it. I'm possessed by the Sugar Plum Fairy." Just to prove it, I started humming this weird song that was a little like the music they play when the Sugar Plum Fairy dances. I mean, I *have* seen *The Nutcracker*. Hasn't everybody?

Cat Poop didn't say anything for a long time. When he did say something, he sounded like he was trying really hard not to be angry. "Do you think I'm stupid, Jeff?"

I shook my head. "No," I said. "You can't be stupid. You went to school in Canada. I hear they have a *way* better education system than we do. Why, do you feel stupid?"

"There are people here who want very much to feel better about themselves," he said, not answering the question. "It's my job to help them do that. It's not my job to sit and listen to you make up a ridiculous story because you don't want to admit that you have a problem."

I pretended to be shocked. "What do you mean?" I said. "I just told you—the Sugar Plum Fairy has taken over my body. She tried to kill me! You have to do something. Like an exorcism. Or a fairycism."

"You're wasting my time," said Cat Poop. "We're done for today."

"What if she tries to make me hurt myself again?" I asked, all concerned. "Or what if she makes me hurt someone else? I might start pirouetting all over the lounge uncontrollably, and I don't know what would happen if I did that. It could be a Sugar Plum massacre."

"Are you finished?" Cat Poop asked.

"That depends," I told him, talking like my normal self again. "Are you ready to let me go home now?"

"You're here for the full forty-five days," said Cat Poop. "You can waste every single one of them if you want to, but you're going to spend them here."

That made me angry. "I thought you said I was wasting *your* time," I snapped.

"You are," he said. "You're also wasting yours, as well as that of someone else who would really like to be helped, who can't be here because you are. I want you to think about that. I'll see you tomorrow."

He looked down, and I knew that was my signal to leave. So I did. And I was happy to get out of there. I couldn't believe he was lecturing *me* about wasting time when he's the one keeping me in this place. All he has to do is say I'm normal and I'll be out of here. If a real whack-job wants my place so badly, I'm perfectly happy to give it up. I'm tired of people thinking they're doing me favors.

Day 07

This morning I went into the lounge and found Sadie writing a letter. When I asked who she was writing to, she said her best friend. "Don't you have a best friend?" she asked me. "You know, someone you tell everything to?"

"Not really," I told her. "I'm not big into friends."

Sadie looked at me funny, then noticed the clock. "I've got to go see Katzrupus," she said, folding up her letter. "See you later?"

"Sure," I told her. "I'm just going to do some homework. Apparently being imprisoned in the cuckoo house doesn't get you out of learning about the reproductive cycle of the frog."

That was another lie. Not the part about homework, the part about not having a best friend. I do, actually. Her name is Allie. I just didn't feel like talking about her with Sadie.

That's right, *her*. Allie is a girl. I know it's kind of weird for a guy to have a girl best friend, but I do.

The first time I saw Allie was when Mrs. Pennyfall, the principal's secretary, walked her into our seventh grade social studies class. Allie stared around the room like she wished she could set it on fire. The only free desk was next to mine, so she had to take it. That whole class, she sat there with her head down, drawing on the cover of her notebook. I kept trying to see what she was drawing, but I didn't want her to think I was staring at her.

Eventually she moved the notebook over a little and I saw what she was doing. The entire cover was covered in perfect little bats. They looked like they were swarming out of the center of the notebook, spiraling around in a big cloud. I couldn't stop looking at them, and Allie noticed. She covered the notebook with her social studies textbook.

After class, I followed her into the hall and told her how cool I thought the bats were. She looked at me and said, "I really don't need any friends, okay? I have enough problems."

"Whatever," I told her. "But you do need someone to show you around. Otherwise you might make the mistake of talking to the wrong people, and then your entire social life will be a disaster."

She looked at me for a moment and then laughed. That's how it started. We had lunch together, and the next day she sat by me in social studies again. I found out she liked some of the things I like—sci-fi movies and roller coasters and some other stuff—and I invited her over to watch *Close Encounters of the Third Kind*, which is the greatest movie ever made, and *way* better than *Star Wars*, no matter what the geeks say. She said okay, and after that we were best friends.

Allie's story is that her mom and dad split up, and her mom moved her to our town because she said it was as far away from Allie's dad as she could get without making it too hard for Allie to see him if she wanted to. Only Allie didn't want to see him, because she was really angry at him for cheating on her mother. That's why they divorced. Allie's mom found out her husband was sleeping with her best friend, which didn't go over very well with her.

Anyway, Allie only sees her dad when she has to, like every other year at Thanksgiving and sometimes in the summer when he decides to pretend they have a relationship and he makes her go on vacation with him and his new wife, who Allie totally hates because she's always trying to get Allie to like her. Her name is Kati—with no e—and she says things like, "Think of me as your big sister," which Allie says makes her want to puke.

Like I said, some people think it's weird that my best friend is a girl. Sometimes I think it's weird, too. Mostly people assume that we're boyfriend and girl-friend, which I guess we could be. But that just seems too teen-movie, if you know what I mean. A boy and girl are best friends, neither of them dates anyone else, and then one night they look at each other and—bang—they realize they've been in love with each other the whole time. Everyone's happy and they go to the big dance together.

Allie and I did go to a dance together once—the spring social in eighth grade—just so we could see what was so thrilling to everyone else. Our mothers made a big deal about it, making us dress up and tak-ing our pictures and all that crap. My mother still has one of the pictures framed and hanging on the wall in our living room. Every time Allie comes over she looks at it and says, "My hair looks like it exploded. Can't you take that down?" But I think secretly she really likes that it's there.

The best thing about Allie is that I can talk to her about pretty much anything. I wish I could talk to her about how I'm feeling right now, about how I hate being in this place with these other people and their weird problems. I know she'd get a laugh out of it all.

I guess I could write it all in a letter, like Sadie, but it's not really the same. I'll wait to tell her everything in person.

I was still thinking about Allie when Sadie came back. I was surprised that a whole hour had gone by already.

"How'd it go?" I asked her.

She said, "You know we're not supposed to talk about our sessions with anyone. Seriously, it might set me back. Do you want to be responsible for that?"

"I'll risk it," I told her.

She slapped my arm. "Thanks for taking my mental health so seriously," she said. "Actually, we talked about my dad."

"What about him?"

Sadie sighed. "Oh, you know, about how I don't think he really loves me and how maybe I was trying to get his attention."

"Were you?"

Sadie looked at her nails, which were chewed down to almost nothing. "Seeing as how he was halfway around the world at the time giving a lecture on medieval architecture, I think I might have planned it a little better if I was," she said. "Once he found out I wasn't dead he waited another week to come home because there was a castle in Spain he wanted to see first."

I wasn't sure I believed her. I mean, a dad who lectures on medieval architecture? That sounds like something I'd make up. But I don't know if Sadie is a liar or not. It's hard to tell with crazy people.

"Do you really think he doesn't love you?" I asked her.

She shrugged. "How do you really know if anyone loves you?"

When I didn't answer, she looked at me. "Really, how do you know?"

I thought about it for a minute. "I guess you just assume they do until they tell you they don't," I said.

Sadie shook her head. "You need a better system than that."

"Maybe you ask," I suggested.

"If you have to ask, the answer is probably no. Do

you think your parents love you?"

I nodded. "Yeah," I answered. "I do. They may be a little whacked, but they love me."

"Do they tell you they do?"

"Sometimes," I said. "My mom more than my dad, but I think that's usually how it goes."

Sadie looked at me for a long time. "You're lucky," she said finally.

I've been thinking about that ever since. Am I lucky? Am I lucky that I didn't die? Am I lucky that, compared to the other kids here, my life doesn't seem so bad? Maybe I am, but I have to say, I don't feel lucky. For one thing, I'm stuck in this pit. And just because your life isn't as awful as someone else's, that doesn't mean it doesn't suck. You can't compare how you feel to the way other people feel. It just doesn't work. What might look like the perfect life—or even an okay life—to you might not be so okay for the person living it.

God, this place is starting to rub off on me. I sound like Cat Poop. I wonder what he would think if I told him about Allie. He'd probably ask me if I'm in love with her.

DAY 08

This is my one-week anniversary at Club Meds. Instead of a party, my big surprise was that my parents came to see me. Or they came because someone told them to, at least. Anyway, when I walked into Cat Poop's office for what I thought was going to be my usual brain-picking session, there they were. At first I thought I was seeing things, or that two people who just happened to look like my parents were there for their own session and I was interrupting. But it was them. They were sitting on the couch.

When she saw me, my mother stood up and started to come toward me, but then stopped. I think maybe Cat Poop had told her not to make any sudden move-

58

ments because they might scare me, like I'm a wild animal or something, because she kept looking at him and then at me. Finally she just said, "Hello, Jeff," and sat down again next to my father.

I sat in the big chair across from the couch and didn't say anything. I mean, really, what do you say to your parents when the last time they saw you, you were practically dead and they had to call the paramedics? It's not exactly your typical "How was school today?" kind of thing. And it's not like we've ever been into the whole sharing thing, anyway. We're not huggers.

"Jeff, is there anything you would like to say to your parents?" Cat Poop said when we'd all been quiet for what seemed like a hundred years.

Is there anything I'd like to say to them? I thought. Yeah, there was. *Why didn't you just let me die?*, for starters. *Why'd you have to come home early from your stupid party? Why'd you have to put me in this place with a bunch of whack-jobs?*

But what I actually said was, "What did you tell everyone?"

My mother rubbed her hands together. "We told Amanda that you were in the hospital," she said. "We didn't tell her why."

"She's thirteen, not four," I said. "She must have

asked." I know my sister. She's got to know everything about everyone. She can tell you which girl at school just got her period for the first time and who's thinking about asking who to the dance. There was no way she hadn't asked them what was going on.

My mom looked at my dad, who looked at the floor. "We told your sister you were having some . . . problems," he said.

I laughed. I don't know why it was funny to me that they hadn't told Amanda the truth, but it was. And I knew they were lying about what they *did* tell her. They must have told her something else. I wondered what she thought was wrong with me. Cancer? A brain tumor? I couldn't wait to find out.

"What about everybody else?" I asked my parents. "What did you tell my school?"

"We told them you were going to be out for a while," my dad said. "That's all."

"Haven't any of my friends called to find out what's up?"

"Amanda has been letting them know that you're sick," said my mother.

"Sick," I repeated. So that's how they thought of me, as being sick. Poor little Jeff, sick and in the hospital while the doctors try to figure out what's wrong with him. The idea of everyone feeling sorry for me made me angry.

"What about Allie?" I asked, surprising myself.

"She hasn't called," my mother said.

I didn't say anything.

"Is there anything the two of you would like to say to Jeff?" Cat Poop asked my parents.

"We love you," my mother said.

I nodded. Like I said before, Hallmark moments aren't my style.

"And we want you to get better," added my father. "So you can come home."

I won't bore you with the rest. There really isn't much more, anyway. Basically, we all sat there for forty-five minutes not saying anything unless the doc made us. Then there was this awkward good-bye part where my mother broke the no-hugging rule and my father patted me on the back. Then they left. Cat Poop had me stay, and when he came back from showing my parents out he asked me how I felt things had gone.

"You could have warned me," I said.

"Why?" he asked. "Did you feel threatened by seeing them?"

"No," I told him. "I just wasn't expecting it, is all."

"Were you embarrassed?"

"It's not like the last time I saw them I was winning the national spelling bee or making the game-winning touchdown or anything," I said.

"Who's Allie?" he asked.

"What?" I said, pretending not to hear him, and kicking myself for saying her name. Of course he was going to jump on that.

"Allie," he repeated. "You asked your parents if Allie had called to ask about you."

"Oh, right. Allie. She's a friend from school."

"Tell me about her."

I shrugged. "There's not much to tell," I said, hoping I sounded casual about it. "She's just a girl I've been friends with for a while."

"But it's important for you to know that she cares what's happened to you." He said it like it was a fact, not a question.

I didn't want to answer him. But he was waiting for me to say something.

"She and I were kind of going out," I said finally. "God, you're nosy. You're worse than my sister."

Cat Poop wrote something on his pad, but didn't say anything. I couldn't tell whether he believed me or not. I wondered how much time was left in our session and prayed it wasn't much.

As if he could read my mind, he put his pen down. "That's all for today," he said. "We'll talk more tomorrow. Oh, and your parents will be coming once a week from now on, so don't say I didn't warn you."

I got out of there as fast as I could, and I've been feeling weird the rest of the day. I don't know why, exactly. Maybe because at first I thought getting out of this place would be a piece of cake. But I think I might have been wrong.

Day 09

Day 9 feels more like Year 100. The worst thing is, I think it's starting to rub off on me. The crazy, I mean. Especially Sadie. I keep thinking about how she tried to kill herself.

That sounds so weird: "kill yourself." It makes it sound like you tried to murder someone, only that someone is you. But killing someone is wrong, and I don't think suicide is. It's my life, right? I should be able to end it if I want to. I don't think it's a sin.

Everyone seems obsessed with it, though. I mean, think about it. We keep people alive on death row just so we can kill them later. We put prisoners on suicide watch so they can't do themselves in before we get the chance to put them on trial. That doesn't make any sense. Why is it okay to put someone to death, but it's not okay for those people to do it themselves?

I'll tell you what I think. I think it pisses people off when you kill yourself because it takes away their chance to control your life, even a little bit. They don't like it when you end things the way you want to and don't wait for the way it's "supposed" to happen. What if suicide *is* the way it's supposed to happen? Do they ever think of that?

I know I'm ranting. It's just that I'm tired of being cooped up in here and having people tell me to talk about my feelings. Like today in group. Cat Poop made us split into pairs and do this stupid exercise where for five minutes one of us had to watch the other one act out what we were feeling. We weren't allowed to say anything; we could only use our bodies and our facial expressions. For five minutes. Then we had to switch and give the other person the chance to let it all out.

Unfortunately, I had to partner with Juliet. She tried to hook up with Bone, like she always does, but Cat Poop asked Bone to pair with Alice. I'd like to have paired up with Sadie, but she got added to the Bone-Alice group because there's an odd number of us. The operative word being *odd*.

Anyway, Juliet seemed as thrilled about the whole thing as I was, looking at me the way she would if the last sandwich on the plate was olive loaf and marshmallow and she had no choice but to take it or starve to death.

"Why don't you go first?" I suggested, and she was totally happy to do it. Big shock. The girl lives to have people pay attention to her. Seriously, I've never met anyone so obsessed with herself.

I sat in a chair and watched while she stood there for a while, I guess thinking about how she was feeling or getting in the mood or whatever. Then she held her hands up like she was holding on to the bars of a cage. She had this sad look on her face, staring at me but not looking at me, if you know what I mean. And she just stood like that for a couple of minutes.

It reminded me of one time when my parents took me to the zoo when I was maybe four or five. I wanted to see the bears, so we went over there and stood with a bunch of other people looking at them. They were brown bears, I remember that, some kind of grizzlies. Everyone was pointing and talking, and the bears were walking around playing with these big plastic balls or sitting in the pool and doing what bears do. All except one. He was sitting in the grass, just looking at the crowd of people. Only he wasn't really looking *at* us, he was looking past us, as if he was trying to see something way off in the distance. I remember how sad he looked, and I remember starting to cry. My parents thought I was afraid, and took me away, but that wasn't it. I was sad. I was sad for that poor bear having to sit in that pen while a bunch of stupid people looked at him and he had to pretend he was someplace else.

That's how Juliet looked, like she could see where she wanted to be but couldn't get there because she was trapped inside something. After a while she put one hand out through the invisible bars, like she was trying to give something to someone. She held it in her palm, like a present. I wanted to reach out and take it, but I remembered that we were just supposed to watch, so I didn't. Instead, I watched her eyes. They were fixed on something behind me. I turned my head to see what it was and saw Bone standing with his back to us. He was watching Alice and didn't see Juliet reaching for him.

I totally don't feel sorry for her now. Bone? How pathetic is that, being so in love with someone who isn't even interested in you? Juliet told us that she's here because she has an eating disorder. I don't know about that. I mean, she's not exactly skinny. I asked Sadie if she's ever heard Juliet yakking up dinner in the bathroom, and she said she hasn't. So we think maybe Juliet's got a bunch of other problems she just hasn't told us about. Yet. I'm sure she will. But really I don't care. If it turns out being in love with Bone is her big problem, I'm going to be really pissed off. What a waste of time.

A minute after I caught Juliet staring at Bone, Cat Poop called out for us to switch, and Juliet sat down without saying anything. I got up and just stood there, not knowing what to do. I felt incredibly stupid. I knew Juliet was waiting for me to do something, but nothing was coming to me. I kept seeing her face, then the bear's face, and then the two faces together, like Juliet was wearing a bear mask or the bear was wearing a Juliet mask.

Then I realized that I couldn't think of anything to do because I really didn't know what I was feeling. All week, I've just been not thinking much about it. Even when I'm talking about it, I'm not really thinking about it. I'm just saying stuff because someone wants me to. I feel like one of the characters in the movie Sadie and I watched the other night, where I'm playing this part but the words that come out of me belong to someone else because the sound is turned off and what I'm saying can't be heard.

That's when I got mad. Mad at my parents for finding me. Mad at myself for not doing it right. Mad at Cat Poop for making me do stupid exercises like standing in front of Juliet looking like an idiot.

So I was just standing there with Juliet watching, and inside of me all of this stuff was whirling around and around like a tornado. But on the outside I was frozen. I couldn't move. So I stood there for the five minutes until Cat Poop told us to stop.

Then it got worse. We had to get together with our partner and talk about what we saw when we looked at each other. I told Juliet that I saw someone who felt trapped, which was a no-brainer. She was all excited, and I knew it wasn't because I'd understood what she was saying, but because she thought she was such a great actress. She kept asking, "Did you like how I" did this and that. I told her she was great, because I figured if I could keep her talking about herself we might never get to talking about me.

I did pretty well, too. When Cat Poop announced that we only had two minutes left, we hadn't said a word about me. I thought I was going to get out of it, only then Juliet looked at me and said, really quick,

"You're hiding something."

I thought she was accusing me of taking something, so I said, "No, I'm not."

"Yes, you are," she said. "There's something inside you that you don't want anyone to see."

And then time was up and group was over. Juliet immediately ran over to see what Bone was doing, and I just sat there. Sadie came and sat next to me.

"How was mime time with Juliet?" she asked me.

"Lame," I said, trying not to think about what Juliet had said to me.

Sadie snorted. "Want to play cards?"

"Do we have to talk about how we feel?"

"Hell no," said Sadie. "In fact, if you say one word about what's going on in there, I'm finding another poker buddy."

That's what I need more of: people who just leave me alone.

Day 10

I couldn't sleep again tonight. I don't know why. I'm pretty used to functioning without the little blue pill now, and it wasn't like I was having bad dreams or anything. I just couldn't sleep. So I went into the lounge, thinking I might finally write Allie that letter after all or maybe help Nurse Moon with her crossword. But Sadie was in there, sitting on the couch and reading a magazine.

"Don't you ever sleep?" I asked her.

"Did you know that only about half of the eggs that get fertilized ever actually turn into babies?" she said, putting down the magazine. "And out of those, only about eighty percent are actually born. The rest get

71

miscarried." She counted on her fingers. "That means out of a hundred fertilized eggs, only forty are ever born."

"Those aren't the best odds," I said.

"And that doesn't include the ones who are born with defects," Sadie added. "That's something like another ten, so ultimately we only have about a thirty percent chance of coming out with no defects."

"I guess it depends what you consider a defect," I told her.

She nodded. "If you look at it that way, there's like a zero chance of being born normal. But think about it: Right from the start the odds are against you. It's kind of amazing that any of us ever get here at all."

"Sort of makes you feel even worse about trying to kill yourself, doesn't it?" I said.

Sadie shrugged. "I hadn't thought about it like that," she said. "But yeah, I guess it does in a way."

"Are you sorry you tried?" I asked her.

She looked out the window. It was snowing. Not hard, just a few flakes. If I'd been at home I would have been hoping for it to turn into a blizzard so that school would be canceled. But when you're locked up, blizzards don't mean much.

"I don't know if I'm sorry or not," Sadie said. "If I

hadn't tried, I'd probably still be sitting around in my bedroom being miserable and writing bad poems."

"I don't think most people would consider that a good deal," I said.

"Maybe not," she told me. "What about you, are you sorry you . . . did what you did?"

"I'm sorry they stopped me," I told her.

"What's so bad about your life?" she said. "From what you've told me about your family, they don't sound so bad."

"They're not," I admitted. "They aren't the problem."

"Then what is?"

"I am," I said. "I'm the problem."

"And what's wrong with you?"

"Nothing's wrong," I said. "I'm just complicated."

Sadie rolled her eyes at me. "Everyone thinks they're complicated," she said. "But actually there are only a couple of things you can have wrong with you. Which one did you get? Low self-esteem? Fear of failure? A martyr complex? Trust me, after three shrinks and a couple of visits to this place, I'm an expert on all of them."

I was surprised to hear her say that. I didn't know she'd been in the hospital before. "I thought this was your first time here," I said.

"Second," she said. "The first time it didn't take, so they sent me back. But we're not talking about me; we're talking about you. So talk."

"I have a better idea," I said. "Let's watch some TV."

I turned the set on and flipped around. Finally I settled on the Lifetime channel, which is always guaranteed to have on some completely idiotic movie about a girl with anorexia, or a woman who gets amnesia and forgets she has an evil twin, or maybe even a family who hires a really creepy babysitter who ends up stalking them. And sometimes you hit the jackpot and end up with a movie that has all of those things in it. And believe me, a movie about an anorexic twin with amnesia who hires a psychotic babysitter is not to be missed.

"Want to play the dialogue game?" I asked Sadie.

"You're on," she said, and I turned the sound off.

We sat and watched the movie for a few minutes until we had the main characters figured out. One was a teenage girl, and the other was an older woman who seemed to be the girl's mother. They were in a diner, eating greasy burgers and arguing about something.

"I'll take the mother," Sadie said. "Alison, I know

you're keeping something from me," she said in what was supposed to be a motherly voice.

Alison is Allie's real name, and for a second I wondered if Sadie had picked it on purpose. But there's no way she could know about her. It was just a freaky coincidence.

"What makes you think I'm hiding something?" I said, trying to sound like an annoyed teenage girl.

"I found your diary," said Sadie. "And I read it."

"How could you!" I said.

"I had to, Alison," Sadie continued. "And I'm glad I did. How else would I have known about . . ."

"About what?" I demanded. "What do you know about?"

"About Chris," said Sadie. "That's right, I know about Chris."

"I was going to tell you," I said.

Sadie shook her head. "I'm so disappointed in you, Alison. How could you not tell me? I'm your mother. If you're seeing a boy, you should talk to me about it."

"Chris isn't a boy," I said, surprised to hear the words come out of my mouth.

Sadie turned and looked at me. "What?" she said.

"Chris isn't a boy," I repeated. "Chris is . . . a girl."

Sadie cracked up. "I didn't see that one coming,"

she said in her real voice. "Good twist. I thought she was just going to be knocked up."

"Yeah, well, you can't go wrong with a teenage lesbian story line," I said. "Had enough?"

Sadie nodded. "I think we've worn this one out. Besides, I'm kind of tired. I'm going to bed. What about you?"

"I'm going to stay up for a while," I said. "I'll see you tomorrow."

After Sadie left I just sat there looking at the television screen. The sound was still off. In the movie, the girl and the woman had gotten into a car and were driving somewhere. They were still arguing. I watched their mouths moving without any sound coming out. And the more I watched them, the more I thought that that's exactly how most people are. They move their mouths, but nothing important comes out. They just talk and talk and talk.

That's what Cat Poop wants me to do: talk. But like I keep telling him, there's nothing to say.

DAY 11

Oh, man, was today weird—the freak show to end all freak shows. It started at breakfast. Today was pancake day, which we have once a week, and everyone was pretty stoked. It's totally queer to get excited about pancakes, I know, but compared to oatmeal and dry scrambled eggs, pancakes are a big deal.

There was sausage, too. That's what started it, the sausage. See, we were all eating, minding our own business and getting lost in the whole syrup sugar-rush thing, when all of a sudden Alice picked up a sausage and started waving it around. She looked like she was conducting an orchestra, moving that sausage up and down to some music only she could hear. The

Sausage Symphony in Nut-job Flat, I guess.

Then she started talking. "This little piggy burned up," she said. "This little piggy burned up. This little piggy went wee-wee-wee, all the way home." Then she laughed, a weird little laugh that sounded like she was strangling.

Juliet was sitting next to her, and she tried to put her arm around Alice and calm her down. But Alice yelled, "Don't touch me! Don't touch the little piggy! I'll burn you up!" Then she giggled some more.

I'm telling you, it was totally bizarre. By that point the nurses had come out, and they were trying to calm Alice down. But the more they touched her, the more she yelled. She just kept yelling, "This little piggy burned up! Wee-wee-wee! Wee-wee-wee!"

The rest of us just sat there and watched. I mean, what else are you going to do? She was totally losing it right in front of us. "Wee-wee-wee! Wee-wee-wee!" And she really did sound like a pig, like she was on fire and squealing in pain.

The nurses finally had to call one of the orderlies to come help them. He pinned Alice's hands behind her back, but she kept right on screaming "Wee-wee-wee!" Only now she was sort of crying-laughing, like she'd completely lost her mind. They dragged her out of the room. Her hair was all wild because she kept shaking her head from side to side. "All the way home," she was saying between squeals. "All the way home."

The weirdest part was that after she was gone everyone else just went back to their pancakes, like nothing had happened. I guess maybe it didn't seem like a big deal because they're crazy too. Maybe this kind of thing happens all the time. But not to me.

"What was that?" I asked Sadie, who was sitting across from me.

She shrugged. "Who knows," she said. "She just snapped."

"Just like that?" I said.

"Sure," Sadie said, like she knew all about it. "The last time I was here, a kid woke up one morning and thought he was Santa Claus. He came out with this pillowcase full of stuff he'd taken from his room, and started handing things out like it was Christmas morning."

Next to her, Bone laughed. "That's excellent," he said.

"It's weird," I said, looking at Bone. It occurred to me today that I have no idea why he's here. I'd ask him, but I really don't care. Besides, there's enough weird to go around as it is. He can keep his to himself.

"Whatever," said Sadie. "Anyway, they'll drug her up and she'll forget all about it." She picked up a sausage and waggled it at me. "Wee-wee-wee," she said. "Wee-wee-wee."

Bone cracked up. "Wee-wee-wee," he said, joining in.

At first I thought it was kind of mean of them to make fun of Alice. But it wasn't like she was there to hear them. And, anyway, maybe that's how nutcases handle things like that. I wouldn't know.

Only Juliet didn't laugh. She just sat in her seat, picking at her pancakes. She had a blank expression on her face, like she was trying really hard not to think about anything at all.

Later on, in group, Cat Poop talked about what had happened.

"Is Alice all right?" Juliet asked him. It was a stupid question. Of course she wasn't all right. She was nuts. But Cat Poop knew what Juliet wanted to hear, because he said, "She'll be okay."

Okay? How can she be okay? She set her mom's boyfriend on fire after he did who knows what to her, she's in a mental hospital, and she thinks she's the piggy who went wee-wee-wee all the way home. That's pretty much the definition of not okay. I shook my head.

"Are you concerned about Alice, Jeff?" Cat Poop asked me.

That was a good question, I'll give him that. I mean, Alice and I weren't friends or anything, but I did feel a little bad for her. After all, it's not her fault she's nuts, right? She had a lot of bad stuff happen to her. But like I said, we weren't friends.

"I just want to make sure what she has isn't contagious," I told Cat Poop.

He pushed his glasses up, so I knew he was annoyed at me. "I think you know the answer to that," he said.

"It's a good question, though," said Sadie. "What if Alice has some sort of virus or something that went to her brain?"

I looked over at Sadie, wondering if she was being serious. She winked at me.

"Alice doesn't have a virus," said Cat Poop.

"But there *are* viruses that can make your brain go all weird, right?" Sadie asked him. "Like Mad Cow."

He sighed. "Yes, there are," he said. "But no one here has a virus."

I gave a fake sneeze. "Uh-oh," I said. "I think I'm coming down with something." Then I oinked.

"I think it's Mad Piggy!"

"Wee-wee-wee," Bone said. Cat Poop looked at him. "Wee-wee-wee," Bone said again. "I think I'm coming down with something too."

Then Sadie started. She fake sneezed and said, "Wee-wee-wee," along with Bone. The two of them were trying really hard not to crack up, and so was I.

Then Juliet stood up. "Shut up!" she screamed at us. "Shut the hell up!"

We did shut up. She's never yelled like that, and it took us by surprise. Juliet glared at us, her hands clenched and her whole body shaking, like she was trying to make our heads explode using the superpowers of her mind.

"Stop making fun of her," she said, really softly. "Just stop. It's not funny." Then she sat down again and looked at the floor.

Maybe she had a point. But come on. Someone yelling about being a little piggy going wee-wee-wee all the way home is kind of funny when you think about it. Sure, I feel bad for Alice, but that's no reason to go all serious. You've got to laugh at stuff.

Anyway, I'm not like Alice. I'm not like the rest of them either. So excuse me if I get a little sarcastic about it when they do something nutty.

Day 12

Alice is gone. Bone told us this morning over break-fast.

"They shipped her out to Morning View," he said between bites of cereal. "I heard the nurses talking about it."

"What's Morning View?" I asked.

"It's where they send all the nuts who are never going to get better," Bone told me. "She's a lifer now. I guess she wee-wee-weed herself all the way to a padded cell."

"And then there were four," said Sadie.

I looked at her. "What?"

"And then there were four," she repeated. "You

83

know, from the nursery rhyme."

She started to recite in a singsong voice.

"Ten little soldier boys went out to dine;
One choked his little self and then there
    were nine.
Nine little soldier boys sat up very late;
One overslept himself and then there were eight.
Eight little soldier boys climbing up to heaven;
One fell down and then there were seven.
Seven little soldier boys chopping up sticks;
One chopped himself in half and then there
    were six.
Six little soldier boys playing with a hive;
A bumblebee stung one and then there were five.
Five little soldier boys on a cellar door;
One fell in and then there were four."

She stopped. "It goes on until they're all dead," she said, spreading butter on a piece of toast. "But right now we still have four."

"What happens to the other four?" Bone asked her.

Sadie took a bite of toast and grinned. "We'll have to see," she said.

"You guys are sick."

It was Juliet. She was sitting a few seats away, her eggs and bacon getting cold on her plate. She hadn't touched them. She was looking at us, and all of a sudden she started to cry.

"Why do you have to be so horrible?" she said.

Sadie put her toast down and wiped her mouth on her napkin before answering her. "Maybe because that's how we deal with it," she told Juliet.

Juliet shook her head. "You're all just afraid," she said. "You're afraid you're going to end up like Alice."

"I'm not," I said before I even realized it. Everyone looked at me. "I'm not going to turn out like Alice," I repeated.

"You already *are* like her," Juliet said. She was staring at my hands, which were resting on the table. Actually, she was staring at my wrists, which were still bandaged. "You just don't know it yet."

I put my hands in my lap. "What I know is that nothing was going to stop Alice from being crazy," I said.

"And what's going to stop you?" Juliet asked me.

To tell the truth, I was getting a little creeped out by Juliet. At first I thought she was just delusional. You know, with the whole Sex and Violence thing, and her crush on Bone. But now I think there's something even more wrong with her. It's like she thinks she can see inside people. She just comes out with this weird stuff, and you can tell she really believes it.

Well, she's wrong about me. She can stare all she wants, but she's never going to see inside me, because there's nothing in there. Everyone could tell that Alice was loony tunes. I'm not blaming her for that or anything, but she was. I, on the other hand, pretty much just had one bad day and now everyone is making me pay for it.

"Don't listen to her," Sadie said. "My guess is that she's the next to go." She gave Juliet a look. "How's it going to happen, Juliet?" she asked. "How are you going to go?"

Juliet stood up and slammed her chair against the table. As she stormed off, Sadie and Bone laughed. After a second, I did too.

"That chick is out there," said Bone.

"Seriously," Sadie agreed. "I wonder what she's in here for. That whole bulimia story was a crock."

"She told me," Bone said. "I guess she thought it might make me love her or something if she shared." He rolled his eyes.

"So?" Sadie said. "Out with it already. What's little Miss Juliet's curse?"

"She's a junkie," said Bone.

"Get out," Sadie exclaimed.

Bone nodded. "No, she is. She was all into heroin and stuff. I guess she ODed a couple of times."

"Wow," Sadie said. "I'm actually kind of impressed. I thought for sure she'd be into something really girly, like cutting herself." Then she looked at me and said, "No offense."

"I didn't realize there was a ranking," I said.

Sadie frowned. "What do you mean?"

"A ranking," I said. "You know, what's crazier than what."

"Oh, sure there is," Sadie said. She sat back in her chair. "First you have your generic depressives. They're a dime a dozen and usually really boring. Then you've got the bulimics and the anorexics. They're slightly more interesting, although usually they're just girls with nothing better to do. *Then* you start getting into the good stuff: the arsonists, the schizophrenics, the manic-depressives. You can never quite tell what those will do. And then you've got the junkies. They're completely tragic, because chances are they're just going to go right back on the stuff when they get out of here."

"So junkies are at the top of the crazy chain," I said.

87

Sadie shook her head. "Uh-uh," she said. "Suicides are."

I looked at her. "Why?"

"Anyone can be crazy," she answered. "That's usually just because there's something screwed up in your wiring, you know? But suicide is a whole different thing. I mean, how much do you have to hate yourself to want to just wipe yourself out?"

"Maybe that's just about wiring, too," I suggested.

"I guess sometimes," Sadie agreed. "But sometimes it's more than that."

"I don't know," Bone said. "I don't see anything so special about wanting to kill yourself." When we didn't say anything, he looked up at us. "Not that I've ever tried it. I'm just saying."

"You're just saying that *because* you've never tried it," Sadie said. She was quiet for a minute, and her eyes got this faraway look in them, like she was remembering something wonderful. "You don't know what it feels like," she continued. "You don't know what it's like to make that decision—to go from thinking about it to doing it. Most people can't do it."

"So you're saying you should get first prize because you did it?" Bone said. He laughed. "You're crazy."

Sadie looked at him. "That's exactly what I am,"

she said, then laughed. "But I'll have to share that prize with Jeff."

She looked at me. "What?" I said.

"You win, too," she said. "You tried to kill yourself, too."

I knew everyone had been thinking that. I mean, how could they not, what with the bandages and everything? But hearing Sadie say it out loud was kind of a shock. I shook my head. "I just did something stupid."

Sadie turned away. "Sure you did," she said.

I couldn't tell if she was making fun of me or not. I sort of don't think she was. And I don't think she wants to share her prize with me. She wants to be Queen Whack-job around here. Or maybe she knows that I'm not like her and the rest of them.

I'm not one of her ten little soldier boys.

DAY 13

One day later and we're back to five. It's like there's a
line of crazies outside, and as one of us leaves they let
in another one. Like at those supposedly cool clubs
where some idiot in sunglasses stands at the door with
a list while a bunch of posers beg him to let them in.
But he only picks the really beautiful people. In this
case, I guess he'd be picking the unbeautiful people.

Anyway, there are five of us again. Well, maybe
four and a half.

I'll explain. This morning at group there was a new
person with us. A girl. At first I thought she was, like,
seven or eight, but it turns out she's twelve. She's so
small and skinny, though, that she looks like a little kid.

Her name is Martha. She sat in her chair hugging a stuffed rabbit. Her arms were wrapped around its middle and her chin rested between its long, floppy ears. She didn't say a word the entire time. Cat Poop told us her name, but that was about it.

I asked him about her later, though, during our session.

"Can't she talk?"

"She can talk," he said. "She just doesn't at the moment."

"Why?" I asked him.

"You know I can't discuss her case with you," Cat Poop said.

"Come on," I prodded him. "How am I supposed to make her feel like one of the family if I don't know anything about her?"

"I notice you've been spending a lot of time with Sadie," he said.

"What do you guys do, spy on us all the time?" I asked. "Or do the nurses secretly film us? Does Nurse Goody have a camera hidden in her hair?"

"Do you feel like we spy on you?" he countered.

This is another therapist trick, answering your question with a question, so that you have to keep talking. I decided to throw it back at him, so I asked,

"Why, do you think I feel like you spy on us all the time?"

Cat Poop actually smiled a little when I did that. "You know we don't," he said. "We keep an eye on you, but we don't spy."

"That's big of you," I said. "It's not like there's much we can do around here, though."

"You seem angry today," he said, ignoring the fact that I was being a smart-ass. "Are you angry?"

Once he asked, I realized that I *was* angry. I hadn't really noticed, but I was. And now I was even more angry because he'd realized it before I had.

"I'm fine," I said.

We sat there for a while with neither of us saying anything. I figured I could probably go the whole session that way, but Cat Poop had other ideas.

"Does Sadie remind you of someone?" he asked me. "Maybe a friend?"

I knew what he was getting at. He wanted to know about Allie. I could have kicked myself for ever having mentioned her around him.

"She's nothing like Allie," I said, just to let him know I knew what he was hinting around about.

"How is she different?" he said.

"Well, for one thing, Allie isn't locked up in a psych

ward," I suggested.

"Is that the only difference?" asked Cat Poop.

"You think I'm in here because of Allie, don't you?" I said.

"I think you're in here because you hurt yourself," he said.

"But you think I did it because of Allie."

"Did you?"

"No," I said.

"Are the two of you close?"

"Can't we talk about my dysfunctional family dynamics?" I suggested. "Or my fear of intimacy?"

"Is Allie your girlfriend?" he asked.

"Can we *please* stop talking about Allie?" I practically shouted. "Jesus, can't you just get over that?"

Cat Poop wrote something down on his stupid pad. I thought maybe he'd finally given up on the Allie questions, but he wasn't done yet.

"Have you and Allie been sexually intimate?"

Like that's any of his business. I wanted to slap him. I hate to admit it, but I'd actually almost started to think old Cat Poop wasn't so bad. But as soon as he asked me that, I knew he was a dirty old man. I mean, he's only like thirty-five or something, but that's old enough to be a dirty old man. The point is, he just wanted to hear about teenagers getting it on.

"What kind of pervert are you?" I asked him. "Can't you just look at some porn? Or do you like hearing people talk about their sex lives?"

He didn't answer the question. I didn't expect him to. I'd caught him, and he was probably embarrassed. He should be. I mean, some stuff is just private.

"How many times do I have to tell you that nothing is bothering me?" I said.

"If nothing is bothering you, then it shouldn't be too difficult to talk about why you tried to kill yourself," said Cat Poop. "Can you do that?"

"Sure," I shot back. "If I wanted to I could. But I don't want to. Not with you."

"Are you saying you'd like another therapist?" he asked me. "I can arrange that if it would help."

I almost told him to go ahead and do it. Then I thought about having to answer the same stupid questions all over again. As annoying as he was being right then, at least I had Cat Poop trained a little bit. If I got a new therapist, I'd be starting all over again.

"No," I said finally. "I don't want a new one."

"I'm honored," said Cat Poop.

"But I'm not talking about Allie, or sex, or anything else that isn't any of your business," I warned him.

"Just so we're clear on that."

"Well, think about what you do want to talk about," he told me. "We'll pick up tomorrow."

"I can't wait," I said as I stood up. "Oh, and by the way, you need a haircut."

As I turned to leave, I saw him reach up and touch his hair. *Score one for Jeff*, I thought as I shut the door behind me.

When I got back to the lounge, the new girl, Martha, was there. She was sitting on the couch, still holding that rabbit in her lap. She was staring out the window at the snow.

I was going to go back to my room, but something made me go over to Martha. She didn't even look at me when I sat down next to her. I kind of wanted to say hello to her. I mean, I know it's not easy your first few days in the nuthouse.

"I like your rabbit," I said.

Martha stopped rubbing the rabbit's ears and looked at me.

"Does he have a name?"

She nodded, but didn't say anything.

"He's your best friend, isn't he?" I said, and she nodded again.

"I have a best friend, too," I told her. "Her name is

Allie, and I tell her everything. Do you tell your bunny everything?"

Martha nodded and held the bunny close to her, like she was protecting him.

"I bet he's a good listener," I said. Then I told her, "You don't have to say anything if you don't want to. We can just sit here together."

She buried her face in her rabbit's fur, but I could see she was smiling. We sat like that for about an hour. I talked about some stuff, nothing important, and she sat there and listened. It didn't matter that she didn't say anything. I think she was happy just having company. I guess having a stuffed bunny for your only friend can get a little lonely.

DAY 14

My bandages came off today. I didn't know they were coming off, so it was a little bit of a shock when Goody Two-shoes called me into the medical room after breakfast and pulled out her scissors. And it was even more of a shock when she unwrapped the gauze and I saw the stitches. I don't know what I thought would be there—maybe some tape or something—but there were little black crisscrosses along my wrists, like tiny railroad tracks. Or animal prints. It looked like a mouse had run across my arm with muddy feet.

The stitches came out, too. That hurt a little, because the skin had healed around them. But Goody's a whiz with her scissors and tweezers, and she got them out pretty quickly. Now I just have these reddish scars there. I guess I always will, although Goody says they'll fade over time.

I don't know if I want them to fade. That probably sounds totally freaky, but part of me doesn't want to forget what it felt like, even though it hurt. If I forget about the pain, I might also forget that it was a really stupid idea to do it in the first place.

My mother told me once that having babies is like that. I guess she was in labor for something like sixteen hours when she had me. Also, it was the middle of July, and being super fat in the hottest part of the year wasn't her idea of fun. All in all, she said, it wasn't as beautiful an experience as they make you think having a baby is, and afterward she told my dad she would never do it again.

But she apparently forgot how much it hurt, because two years later she had my sister. Although that time she planned it so she'd be her fattest in the winter, when she could wear a bunch of clothes to cover it and she wouldn't mind being warm all the time. And she had them load her up on painkillers the minute she started having contractions. Amanda only took, like, two hours to pop out, anyway, a fact my mother reminds me of whenever she wants to make me feel guilty. Then I remind *her* that nobody told her to go and get pregnant.

Not that I'm really comparing having kids to trying to kill yourself. I'm just saying that sometimes forgetting how much things hurt makes you do them again. And that's not always such a hot idea.

I'm not even sure I want kids, by the way, even if I'm not the one who has to be pregnant. It seems too risky. I mean, what if you end up with a kid that's just plain bad? Or stupid? It's not like you can give it away or put it in a garage sale or something. You're pretty much stuck with it for a long time.

I know now they have all these tests they can do so you can find out if your kid has three arms or is retarded or whatever, but you can't test for everything. You can't test for crazy, for example, or for bad taste in music and clothes and stuff. You can't know if your kid is going to be someone you would actually want to have hanging around. You just have to take your chances. That seems like a pretty big gamble to me.

Not that I'd be having any kids right away, anyway. I'm only fifteen. I know, there are a lot of fifteen-year-olds out there having babies, but not me. I don't need to mess up my life any more than it already is. So no babies for me. I'm glad we got that straightened out.

I don't know how I got from my stitches to babies. Sometimes my mind goes in weird directions. Or maybe it's the meds, which I'm still on. But Cat Poop says these are just antidepressants, and nothing too heavy-duty. Not like the Pez.

Anyway, after I got my stitches out, I went to show Sadie. I know I kind of freaked out the other day when she mentioned them, but the truth is, she's really the only person who hasn't treated them like they're a big deal, and that's sort of cool.

She asked if she could touch my scars, and I said it was okay. She ran her fingers over them like they were puppies, really softly, like she was afraid she might open them up again.

"I don't have any scars," she said, and she sounded kind of sad.

"Do you remember almost drowning?" I asked her. It's something I'd been wondering for a while, but I wasn't sure it was something I should ask. Now, since she was touching my scars and all, well, I figured it was as good a time as any.

"I remember everything was green and quiet," she said. "At first—when the air ran out—my chest burned. But then the pain went away, and everything was really quiet. I felt like I was flying. The next thing

I remember is lying on the grass. Sam was breathing into my mouth and all these people were staring at me."

I asked her who Sam was, and she said he was the guy who'd saved her. He'd seen her jump into the lake with all her clothes on, and he'd thought it was a little weird. When she went under and didn't come up, he jumped in and pulled her out again.

"He's called a couple of times," Sadie told me. "You know, to see how I am."

After that I had to go see old Cat Poop. The first thing I noticed was that something about him looked different. "You got a haircut," I said once I realized what it was.

"Yes," he said.

I wanted him to say that I'd been right about his needing to deal with his hair, but instead he launched right into therapy time. He reminded me that my parents were coming tomorrow for their weekly visit. Then he asked me how I was getting along with the other kids. I told him I was getting along fine, and he seemed happy with that.

I thought things were going too easily. Then Cat Poop said, "I see your bandages are off."

Like he didn't know. I'm pretty sure Goody would

never have removed them without his permission. I looked down and said, "I guess they are," like until then I hadn't even noticed. "How about that?"

"How do you feel about seeing the cuts?" he asked me.

I shrugged. "I guess it means my career as a hand model is over," I said. "That might take some getting used to."

The doc looked at my face for a long time, so I said, "Seriously, it doesn't bother me. They're just cuts."

I think he was trying to figure out how big of a lie I was telling. The thing is, I wasn't telling one at all. Seeing the cuts really doesn't bother me. Honestly, it's better than having your wrists wrapped up like a mummy. Besides, as long as I wear long sleeves forever, I'll hardly ever see them.

"All right," Cat Poop said, but I don't think he was totally convinced. "Then that's it for today."

All in all, it was a pretty good day. For one thing, I got Cat Poop to cut his hair, which I think is a totally huge achievement. Plus, I got my bandages off and didn't freak out about it. I think I can honestly say that for the first time since I got here, I'm feeling more or less okay.

Day 15

So my parents came again today. This time things went much better. At least I think they did. The only weird thing was that my mother kept staring at my wrists. Somehow I'd forgotten about the scars already and I wore a T-shirt. I tried to cross my arms and tuck my hands in, but I was afraid they'd think I was being hostile, so instead I just clasped my hands together and tried to keep the scar sides in. Still, she kept looking down there.

   Cat Poop started off the session by asking my parents each to name one thing about me that they were proud of. You can imagine how excited I was about that, but actually it wasn't too cringe-inducing. My father said that he's always been proud of the fact that I do well in school, which is a pretty dad thing to say, very neutral and not too touchy-feely. My mom said she was proud of everything I did. Cat Poop asked her to be more specific, which made me want to laugh (but I didn't), and she said she guessed she was most proud of the fact that I was a good person.

I'm not sure what a good person is, exactly. On the one hand, it could be someone who always plays by the rules. But someone can follow the rules and still be a real jerk, you know? In fact, some of the biggest idiots I know are people who follow the rules, usually because they make you feel like crap when you don't.

Or maybe a good person is someone who's always doing good things for other people. That sure isn't me. I'd probably get kicked out of Boy Scouts if I was in it because I wouldn't help old ladies across the street, if you get my drift. Not that I'm a jerk or anything; it's just that other people aren't always my main priority in life.

I kind of wish Cat Poop had asked my mom to be even more specific, but I think he thought she'd done the best she could. Instead, he asked me to tell my parents two things about them that I was thankful for. I thought it was a little unfair making me say *two* things when they'd had to come up with just one each, but I gave it a shot.

First I said I was thankful that they always made sure I had everything I needed, like clothes and food and a house. Second, I said I was thankful that they never made me feel bad about myself. I was thinking about Sadie when I said that, about how her dad always made her feel like she was a problem. I also thought about Alice and her mother's boyfriend. I still have a hard time believing that any mom would let that happen to her kid, even though you read about it in the paper and see it on the news all the time. Until I met Alice, I always assumed it happened to "other" people, as in people I didn't know. I guess there are a lot more other people than I thought there were.

After we talked a little more, they said they had a surprise for me. Amanda was with them. Cat Poop wanted to talk to my parents some more, so he told me to go into the room next to his office, which it turns out is almost exactly like his office except there's no picture of a dog carrying a dead bird. I guess it's for another shrink, although it looked like no one had used it in a long time.

Amanda was waiting there. When I came in she jumped up and gave me a big hug.

"Watch it," I told her. "First mom, and now you. This hugging stuff is starting to scare me."

"You jerk," she said, but not in an angry way. "You scared me. Don't ever do that again."

I still wasn't sure how much she knew about why I was in the hospital, so I was a little nervous. Again, I tried to hide my wrists by sticking my hands in the pockets of my jeans.

"It's okay," Amanda said. "They told me. Besides, it's not like you could hide the bloodstains on the carpet. There was a *lot* of it."

"They let you see it?" I asked.

She shook her head. "I snuck in. At first they tried to tell me you sliced yourself opening a CD with a box cutter."

She rolled her eyes, and I laughed. That's totally something my parents would do. I could just see Amanda demanding to know the real story.

"Are you really okay?" she asked me.

"Sure," I said. "I'm fine."

She gave me a look like she didn't believe me, but she didn't say anything. I knew she wanted to believe that everything's all right, and even though she probably had a million other questions, she didn't ask any of them then.

Then I noticed her hair.

"I dyed it," Amanda said.

"No kidding," I said.

Had she ever. Her hair is naturally this kind of blondish red, just like my dad's. Now it was a lot more red. In fact, it was *really* red. Like a cherry Popsicle.

"Relax," she said when I didn't say anything for a minute. "It's just Kool-Aid. But don't tell Mom. She thinks it's permanent."

I laughed. It felt good. I hadn't had a real laugh since I woke up in the hospital. "I won't," I promised. "Why are you torturing her this time?"

Amanda shook her head. "No reason," she said. "It's just fun."

That's what I love about my sister. She does things just because she wants to. I know you're not supposed to think your little sister is cool, but by now I think it's pretty obvious that I don't exactly do things by the book.

Amanda sat down on the couch, and I sat in a chair across from her. "What's the word around school?" I asked her. My heart raced a little as I waited for her to answer. I don't really care what people think about me most of the time, but disappearing and ending up in the hospital are a little more serious than breaking out in zits or wearing the wrong sneakers.

"That depends who you ask," said Amanda. "The popular theory is mono, although I've also heard that you have cancer, hepatitis, and maybe a brain tumor. Oh, and for about a day and a half you'd run away because mom and dad caught you doing drugs."

"Excellent," I said. "Does anyone know the real reason?"

"If they do, they didn't hear it from me," she told me. "I'm sticking with mono."

Then I asked her the one question I was really interested in hearing the answer to. "Have you seen Allie around?"

"Yeah," Amanda said. But there was something in her voice that sounded weird, as if she really didn't want to talk about it. So of course I made her.

It turns out Amanda saw Allie at lunch about a week after I came to the hospital. She thought Allie would want to know that I was okay, even if she couldn't tell her exactly what had happened, so she went over to her and started talking.

"But all she did was kind of nod," Amanda said. "She was sitting with this guy, and it was like she didn't really want to talk to me."

I told Amanda that we'd had a fight about something, but that it wasn't a big deal and Allie would get over it. I know Amanda didn't buy it, but for once she let it go. Like I said, she's pretty cool. Not that I'd ever let her know that. I have to keep her in line somehow or she'll think she's the boss of everything.

"Anyway, you've got to get out of here soon," said Amanda. "They're driving me nuts."

I knew she meant my mother and father. I could just imagine what they were like to live with now. I'm surprised they hadn't installed security cameras in Amanda's room. And now her Kool-Aid hair made even more sense. Knowing Amanda, she'd done it just to *make* them worry.

"Sorry about that," I said. And I really was. I mean, it's not Amanda's fault that I'm in here.

"I can handle it," she assured me.

We just sat there for a minute, like we'd run out of things to say. But it wasn't awkward or weird. It was kind of nice. Amanda was treating me the way she always does, not like I'd done something crazy. Then Cat Poop opened the door and my parents came in. I don't know what he said to them, but they were all smiling again, like circus clowns. I wanted to hand them some balloons.

"We'll see you next week," my mother said. She

looked like she was going to hug me again, but I moved so that Cat Poop was between us and just said, "Okay. See you then."

No one else tried to hug me, although I know Amanda would have if my parents hadn't been there, and that would have been okay. They all said good-bye and left. I'm sure they were as happy to get out as I would have been if I was leaving with them.

It made me think of Mrs. Christensen. Mrs. Christensen is about seventeen million years old. She's a friend of my grandmother's, and she lives in a home now because her entire family is dead. Every Christmas we have to go visit her. We take her a fruit-cake and some presents, like slippers and chocolate and whatever. We spend about an hour with her, and it's the longest hour in the history of time. The home smells like old people, and even though they put up all of these decorations, it's still depressing. Mrs. Christensen always acts like we're her real family, but we aren't, and I can't wait to get out of there.

I bet that's how my parents and Amanda feel. I know I would if one of them was in here. I'd just want to get it over with and leave the fruitcake.

Day 16

Before my parents left yesterday they gave me a care package from my grandmother. Actually, they left it with Cat Poop, and he gave it to me today. They probably had to run it by the drug-sniffing dogs or something to make sure there was nothing in it I'm not supposed to have. Like my grandma would have stuck packets of heroin in there. Or porn.

Anyway, she sent me chocolate chip cookies, some peanut butter fudge, and a dollar. She always puts a dollar in when she sends me or my sister something—cards, letters, whatever. It must be an old lady thing to do. My dad says she always gave him and his brother a dollar when she wrote to them, too, until they had kids of their own. Now she sends us the dollars. I guess she figures my dad doesn't need them.

I shared the cookies and fudge with everyone else, but only because I knew that otherwise I'd just eat it all and then feel sick. Besides, we had movie night tonight. They let us watch a DVD of a movie about this guy who spent every summer living with grizzly bears in Alaska. It's a true story. Every year he hiked into the wilderness and followed the bears around until fall came and they went into hibernation. Until one year when a bear ate him.

You'd think it would be all sad, someone being eaten by a bear. The thing is, though, this guy really loved those bears. He loved everything about them, even when they did stuff that looked totally mean, like fight over food or kill a rival bear's cubs. It was like they were his family, and he forgave them for their bear behavior because he knew they couldn't help it. I think he probably even would have forgiven the bear that ate him.

They interviewed a lot of people in the movie, and most of them said they just couldn't understand why this guy would want to spend so much time with bears. Some of them thought he believed he was a bear because he couldn't handle who he really was. I think they're wrong. I think he just loved being with the bears because they didn't make him feel bad.

I mean, sure, this guy was a little nuts. You'd have to be to spend your whole life following bears around. But I get it, too. When he was with the bears, they didn't care that he was kind of weird, or that he'd gotten into trouble for drinking too much and using drugs (which apparently he did a lot of). They didn't ask him a bunch of stupid questions about how he felt, or why he did what he did. They just let him be who he was.

I guess if you think about it, it was kind of a strange movie for them to let us watch. But I think that a lot of us in here could relate to it. Juliet started to cry when they talked about how rangers shot the bear that ate the guy and then cut it open to make sure he was really inside. Personally, I think they killed the bear because they were afraid of it. That's what people do, kill the things they're afraid of.

Here's what I think. One, people should figure out that if they go around bothering bears, chances are they're going to end up bear snacks. Second, people suck.

There I go again, jumping from fudge to bears. I swear, sometimes it feels like there's this monkey in my head who runs around turning the dials and changing channels on me. One minute I'm sitting around eating chocolate chip cookies and then all of a sudden I'm thinking about bears.

Like I said, though, I think a lot of us relate to those bears. We're in here because someone—our parents, our doctors, the people who supposedly love us—are afraid of us. We're in the Whack-job Zoo so that everyone can look at us without getting close enough to get hurt. Man, that's messed up.

I wonder what Cat Poop would do if next time he starts nosing around in my brain, I just bite him?

Day 17

Alert the media: Martha spoke to me today.

I was sitting with her on the couch, reading, and out of nowhere she put her hand on my wrist and said, "Frex."

I was so shocked that I stopped reading and just looked at her. She touched my wrist again. "Frex," she said, like she was telling me the name of something.

"Frex," I said, and she nodded. Then she touched her chest and said it again.

At first I thought I should call for Cat Poop, but then I decided it might scare Martha if I got all excited. So I waited, and she rubbed her fingers along the cuts on one of my wrists. "Frex," she said. "Frex."

I didn't know if she was talking about my wrist, my cut, or nothing in particular. It was sort of like a scene in one of those sci-fi movies where a human and an alien are trying to communicate and neither really knows what the other is saying. Like the alien says "Frex," and the human doesn't know if it means "Don't worry, I won't hurt you" or "I've laid an egg in your stomach and it's about to hatch, so kiss your butt good-bye."

Martha touched her chest again, where her heart is, and repeated herself a couple of times—"frex, frex, frex"—just like that. She said it almost like she was singing a song.

That's when I got it. All of a sudden it made sense. She was talking about hurting. My scar and her heart. Whatever "frex" is to her, it means something that hurts. Who knows how she came up with that word. I guess it doesn't really matter. It's her word, and now I know what it means.

That's all that happened. There wasn't any big emotional scene or anything. Martha didn't all of a sudden tell me her life story and solve the mystery of why she doesn't talk. But it was kind of cool anyway.

Later on I told Cat Poop what had happened. I thought he'd jump up and down and push his glasses up, but he just smiled and nodded.

"Did you already know?" I asked him, but he shook his head.

"No," he said. "You should be proud of yourself. She opened up to you."

"Why should I feel proud?" I asked him. "I didn't do anything. She's the one who did the talking."

"You let her know it was okay to tell you," he said.

Whatever. I hate to rain on his parade, but I didn't do anything. I'm not going to get all excited about her saying "frex." I still don't know why she would talk to me and not other people. But how weird is it that she made up that word? Frex. Hurt. I guess she was saying that her heart hurts because of what happened to her. I wonder if she'll ever really be able to talk about it, or if she's so inside herself that this is as good as it gets. Like Alice.

In other news, I forgot that Allie's birthday was yesterday. Not that it's really my fault. You don't exactly keep track of the date so well around here. The days all kind of run into each other, like one big long one that never ends. But today I happened to look at the date on the newspaper at the nurses' station and realized I'd missed Allie's birthday. She turned sixteen. I'll be sixteen this summer, so she's got half a year on me. That never bothered her, though. She always called herself "the older woman."

I wonder what she did for her birthday. Actually, I don't wonder at all. I know what she did. She spent it with Burke. He's her boyfriend. He probably took her to the movies or maybe out for pizza. I bet he bought her some stupid present she normally wouldn't even like, and I bet she gushed over it like it was the best thing ever.

It makes me sick how she gets all stupid over him. She was never like that before. She never let a guy turn her into something she's not. Then Burke came along and everything changed. Everything.

I don't get how someone can become a different person overnight, but Allie did. It was like there was this whole other girl living inside of her, and one night that girl broke through and took over. One day we were doing everything together, and the next everything was over. She just threw it all away.

The worst part is, you know they're not going to be together forever. I mean, come on, she's fifteen. Okay, sixteen. Still. It's not like they're going to get married or anything. Even if they last a couple of years—which they won't—she'll go to one college and he'll go to another, and pretty soon they'll forget all about each other. That's what always happens. That's why teenage dating is so dumb, because it's doomed to fail. You'd think people would have learned that by now, but I guess they haven't. They go right on falling in love and thinking it's going to survive high school. Allie and Burke, true love always.

Whatever.

Anyway, happy birthday, Allie. I hope it was a good one.

Day 18

As Sadie says, "And then there were four." Again.

Today in group Cat Poop announced that it was Bone's last day in the program. When he said it, Juliet's face kind of fell, but she didn't say anything. I don't think she's been quite so excited about him since he made fun of Alice.

Good for Bone that he's getting out, I guess. I know he's a little scared about it, because he said so in group. I was really surprised that he said anything. I mean, we've talked some, but it's not like he's ever said very much about himself. But today he did.

It turns out his parents don't want him to come home. They don't think they can trust him not to get into trouble. As usual, he didn't explain what kind of trouble he meant. But by now I'm used to not knowing anything about Bone, and I didn't ask. Nobody did. I think we like that he's our Mystery Man. It means we can make up whatever story we want about him.

Anyway, he's going to stay with his older brother and his brother's wife. They live in a little town somewhere in Arizona and own a gas station. Bone's going to work at the gas station until he figures out what he wants to be when he grows up. That's not what he's afraid of, though. He's afraid that people will find out about him being in a psychiatric hospital and think he's some kind of criminal or something. He's afraid they'll tell their kids to stay away from him and cross the street when they see him. "Don't talk to the crazy man, honey. He might bite you."

Coming from someone covered in tattoos, this seemed a little strange. I mean, you can *see* tattoos. You can't see crazy. If I was him, I'd be more worried about people thinking he was in a gang or something.

Later, after my session with Cat Poop, I went into the lounge. Bone was in there watching a talk show, one of those with a host so perky you want to slap her. The topic was people who wanted to make over their friends who they thought looked too weird.

One of the girls on the show wanted her sister to stop dressing like what she called a punk. She said people made fun of her when she went outside, and that people thought she was a Satan worshipper and stomped on kittens or something. The host kept frowning and shaking her head. Then they brought the girl out. She was totally Goth. Her hair was all black, and she had on pancake makeup and blood red lipstick. She was a little overweight, and she looked like Robert Smith from the Cure. I thought she was kind of cute.

As soon as she came out, the audience started booing, like she'd murdered her best friend or slept with her dad's new wife. Then the host asked her why she dressed like she did, and she said, "Because I like to." The audience booed again, and her sister screamed, "People think she's a lesbian!" The Goth girl covered her face with her hands like she was all embarrassed.

Then they went to a commercial, and when they came back from telling us about how fresh we'd all feel if we used panty shields with wings, they'd done the makeovers. They hauled out all of these people whose friends thought they looked too strange, and now they all looked like they'd been trapped inside a J.Crew store for a night and come out different people.

They saved the Goth girl for last, and when they brought her out she was wearing this flowered dress and big dangly earrings and Mary Jane shoes. When her sister saw her, she started crying, and the audience gave her this standing ovation because she didn't look freaky anymore. When she sat down, the host flashed this series of pictures of her, starting with her baby picture and going on up until high school. The audience oohed and aahed at how pretty she was as a little girl—all blonde curls and wide eyes. Then the last photo was of her all Gothed-out, and the audience hissed.

The Goth girl looked really unhappy, and the host asked her if she liked her new look. She said she hated it, and everyone got really angry, like they'd paid for the makeover themselves. Then this guy stood up and said, "I'd never ask you out looking the way you looked before."

The girl looked at the guy for a minute, and then she said, "What makes you think I'd ever *want* someone like you to ask me out." Then she turned to her sister and said, "So, now that I look like this, I'm okay? I'm not a freak because I look like you do? Well, you can go fuck yourself." Only of course they bleeped out the good part because it's daytime TV, and we all know that no one in America swears.

The guy she'd talked back to just stared at her like she'd kicked him in the balls, and her sister was crying her eyes out. The girl looked at them both and said, "What a bunch of losers." Then she walked off the set. The host started smiling again, and they cut to a commercial for pork, the other white meat.

It was great. Bone and I were dying. Then Bone said, "Jesus Christ, people still think what you look like is who you are."

I looked at the tattoos up and down his arms. I'd seen them before—you can't miss them—but I'd never really *looked* at them. When I did, I saw that between the flaming skulls and hearts were the characters from *Alice in Wonderland*. He has the Red Queen and the Dormouse on one arm and the Mad Hatter and March Hare on the other one. One forearm has that picture of Alice with her neck all stretched out from eating the magic mushroom.

"Is that who you are?" I asked Bone, pointing to Alice.

He laughed. "No," he said, "This is who I am." He lifted his shirt, and on his back was the White Rabbit, wearing his waistcoat and looking at his watch. It was just like the illustration from the book. Only standing next to him, back-to-back, was another White Rabbit wearing a leather motorcycle jacket and boots and smoking a cigar.

"That's me," said Bone. "Always running. Always late. I had it put on my back because no one can see it unless I show it to them. The ones on the outside are for people to stare at. But I keep the one I really love hidden."

"Why two of them?" I asked him.

"Yin and Yang," he said. "Dark and light. One's the good rabbit and one's the naughty rabbit."

"Which one is which?" I asked.

He laughed again. "Both," he said. "It's kind of a bipolar thing. Like me." Then he got up and left before I could ask him anything else, just like the Rabbit does to Alice.

I sat there for a while thinking about the Goth girl. Actually, I was thinking about the opposite of her—how people think that if you look "normal," then you are.

One time Allie and I skipped school and went to see this foreign film called *Los Diablos*, where these villagers found a glowing blue ball and peeled pieces off of it to see what was inside. Only the ball was really radioactive, and they all died from the poison. I think that's what happens when you look too deep inside for the truth. The poison comes out, and you die, even though you have beautiful glowing pieces of blue truth in your fingers.

And anyway, the truth isn't all that great. I mean, what's the truth? Planes falling out of the sky. Buses blowing up and ripping little kids into millions of pieces. Twelve-year-olds raping people and then shooting them in the head so they can't tell. I can't watch the news anymore or look at the papers. It's like whoever sits up there in Heaven has this big bag of really crappy stuff, and once or twice a day she or he reaches in and sprinkles a little bit of it over the world and it makes everything go crazy, like fairy dust that's past its expiration date.

Day 19

I woke up this morning to a snowstorm. A full-blown
blizzard. It's so white outside my window it looks like
the hospital is flying through the clouds. It's beautiful.
The snow just keeps coming and coming. Those crazy
naked trees I can see from my room look like they're
juggling cotton balls.

Goody and the other day nurse couldn't get in
because the roads aren't plowed, so Nurse Moon and the
rest of the night shift had to stay on, and they were not
happy about it. They just wanted to go home and get
some sleep. Cat Poop couldn't make it in either, so basically we all had the day off. We were making the staff
crazy because we were so hyped-up about the snow.

It was Sadie's idea to go outside. Juliet said something about how the snow looked perfect for making snowmen, and the next thing you know, Sadie was asking if we could all go out in it for a while.

At first Nurse Moon said no. But then the other night nurse (Nurse McCutcheon, who always looks like she's forgotten something but can't remember what it is) said she would supervise us. Then Moon said it was okay, as long as two attendants went with us and we all stayed in a group.

I haven't been outside since I came here. We can't even open the windows more than a couple of inches. So I was excited about getting away from the stuffy rooms for a while. Only then I remembered that I didn't have any outside clothes with me. My parents had brought me some jeans and shirts and stuff, but no boots or coat or anything. I mean it's not like we go on nature hikes or anything. No one else had any either.

It turns out the hospital had some. I don't know if they were left over from other patients or what, and I didn't want to ask. I mean, if they were, why did they leave them behind? That's the kind of question that really doesn't have any good answer.

Anyway, we bundled up in the coats and scarves and mittens and stuff. Not everything fit us exactly right, but it was good enough. My only gripe is that the coat they found for me was bright yellow. Like some dog had peed in snow. But hey, it's not like I was shopping at Macy's.

Once we were dressed, we filed downstairs. We had to go through two sets of locked doors, and it felt like we were prisoners being transferred from one jail to another. But finally we made it out into the big square formed by the four wings of the hospital. As soon as we were in the yard, Sadie scooped up a bunch of snow, made a snowball, and threw it at Juliet. It hit her in the back of the head, exploding into a million flakes. Juliet made her own snowball and threw it back at Sadie. Only she missed and hit one of the attendants.

That was all it took. Within seconds it was a full-on snowball war. There were no teams or anything; it was everyone for themselves. We didn't have anything to hide behind, so basically we just kept making snowballs and throwing them at whoever was closest.

I thought for sure Nurse McCuthcheon would make us stop, but she just got out of the way and watched, with a little smile on her face. I made a mental note to be nicer to her from now on. Not that I've given her any trouble, but you know what I mean. I could be less of a pain sometimes.

I pegged one of the attendants in the back, and while I was laughing at him, I got hit in the side of the face myself. I turned to see who had thrown the snowball, and I saw Martha smiling from ear to ear.

After we were all worn out from the snowball fight, Juliet started making that snowman she'd been talking about. She made a small ball of snow and then pushed it across the yard, making it bigger. Sadie and I helped her, making smaller balls for the middle and head of the snowman. Martha stood watching us but not joining in.

I went over to her and said, "You want to see an angel?"

She looked up at me with those big eyes and nodded. I walked over to a part of the yard we hadn't trampled on yet and lay on my back in the clean snow. I moved my arms and legs up and down in a jumping-jack motion, then stood up, leaving an imprint.

"See," I told Martha. "It's a snow angel. Do you want to make one?"

She nodded and threw herself into the snow. She kicked her arms and legs crazily, then got up. Her angel was a little lopsided, like it had fallen out of Heaven or something, but it looked really cool. Martha laughed when she saw it. I think it was the first time I'd ever heard her laugh. It sounded like Christmas.

"Let's make some more," I told Martha.

We lay in the snow next to each other and made our angels. I was going to get up, but Martha took my hand and held it. She was wearing these red mittens they'd found for her, and I could feel her fingers gripping mine through my gloves. We just stayed like that, looking up at the sky while the snow came down. It kept falling, and for a little while it felt like we were flying through space and the snowflakes were stars rushing all around us.

That made me think about the astronauts again, about how the air on Earth smells so bad to them. I took a deep breath and filled my chest with the cold air. It didn't stink. It smelled great for a change.

Martha and I finally got up and helped the others finish the snowman. We'd brought a carrot for his nose, and Nurse McCutcheon had gotten us two cookies to use for his eyes. Juliet took off the purple scarf she'd found in the clothes closet and wrapped it around the snowman's neck.

"What are we going to name him?" Sadie asked when he was done.

"How about Frosty?" Juliet suggested.

"Too obvious," said Sadie. "It should be something unique. Like him."

"How about Cat Poop," I said.

Sadie laughed, but Juliet looked confused. "I don't get it," she said.

Neither Sadie nor I enlightened her. Sadie's the only person I've told about my special name for the doc, and I kind of like that it's our secret.

"What about Bone?" said Juliet.

"What about him?" Sadie replied.

"The snowman," Juliet said. "Why don't we call him Bone? Or Boney. Like Frosty but different."

Sadie raised one eyebrow. "Boney the snowman," she said. "It's ironic." She looked at Juliet. "And fucked up. I like it."

Juliet grinned. Sadie turned to me and Martha. "Are we all in agreement?" she asked.

I nodded, and so did Martha.

"Then Boney it is," Sadie said. "Welcome to the world, Boney."

We stood around looking at Boney for a while. Then Juliet started humming. A few seconds later, she started singing to the tune of "Frosty the Snowman."

"Boney the snowman, was a crazy, whacked-out guy, with tattooed skin and a goofy grin, and he liked to get real high."

Sadie and I laughed. Then Sadie sang some more.

"There must have been some acid in the soda that he had, 'cause when he went and drank it, it screwed him up real bad."

"Excellent," I said, applauding the two of them.

"Your turn," said Sadie.

I thought hard, trying to remember another verse of the Frosty song. It had been a long time since I'd sung it. It took a moment, but then I sang, badly, "He led them to the psycho ward, right to the dear old doc. And when they asked him what was wrong, he told them . . ." I couldn't think of how to end it.

"Suck my cock," Juliet said. "He told them, 'suck my cock.'"

Sadie turned and high-fived her. It was exactly what Bone *would* have said. Then all of us threw ourselves into the snow, laughing so hard I was afraid Nurse McCutcheon would think we were having fits. Even Martha did it, although I don't think she really got why our song was funny.

After that we all went back inside, took off our snowy clothes, and sat in the lounge drinking hot chocolate, just like those goddamn perfect families you see in holiday commercials.

Day 20

I've got a little bit of a cold today from being outside in the snow yesterday. That's okay, though, because it was totally worth it to get out of here for a while. When I looked out the window this morning, I saw Boney still standing in the yard. There was a cardinal sitting on his head, picking at the carrot, and something—probably squirrels—had taken the cookies during the night. But he still looked pretty good. He was still holding up.

Even better: I'm not the only guy anymore. There's another one. I guess the person who controls the guest list decided we needed a new face at our party.

Anyway, his name is Rankin. He's a big guy, pretty normal looking. He reminds me of the guys who play football at school, the ones who think they rule the place because they can toss a ball around. I'm not a big fan of the jocks, I have to tell you. It's like God knows they're going to have crappy lives when high school is over and nobody cares anymore that they can score a goal or touchdown or whatever, so he makes them the big heroes for a few years to make up for it. The only problem is, the rest of us have to put up with them, which is totally not fair.

"Yeah," he said when Cat Poop introduced him. "I'm Rankin. Hey." He lifted one hand and sort of waved at us, then quickly put it back in his lap and gave a stupid half grin, as if he knew how dumb he looked.

Cat Poop waited a moment for him to say something else, but he didn't. Watching Rankin, I wondered if I'd looked as clueless on my first day there as he did. Now I was a veteran. An old-timer. I also wondered if he was looking at me and thinking that I was crazy, the way I'd looked at Sadie, Bone, and the others that day.

"Is there anything you'd like us to know about you, Rankin?" the doc finally asked.

"Oh, right," Rankin said, as if his brain had just been on pause and Cat Poop had hit the play button. "I play football."

I laughed, just a little bit, but everybody heard it and looked at me. Rankin's eyebrows went all scowly and he said, "What?"

"Nothing," I said. "It's just that I was thinking you look like a jock."

He smiled. "Oh," he said. "Yeah, I am." I guess he thought I was complimenting him. Anyway, he was quiet for a few seconds, like he was trying to decide what to say. Then he said, "I just get kind of down sometimes."

I almost laughed again. He sounded like such a little kid. "I get down sometimes." Yeah, probably because it's so hard being a popular jock and having everyone fall all over themselves whenever you win a stupid game. What an idiot.

Still, it's kind of nice not being the only guy. Even though it was only for a day, I definitely felt outnumbered after Bone left. I was sort of afraid Juliet, Sadie, and Martha were going to make me play house with them, or have a tea party, or paint our toenails. Not that I think Rankin and I will be best buds or anything.

I wonder what he's in for. I know—he gets sad

sometimes. Who doesn't? But there's got to be something more going on in that big head of his. I'd try to figure it out, but, honestly, I really don't care. Crazy is crazy. You either are or you aren't. Like they are and I'm not. It's pretty simple.

I've kind of given up trying to convince Cat Poop that I'm not. After all, I've been here three weeks tomorrow. That's almost half of my sentence. Clearly, they aren't letting me out early for good behavior. So now I just go to my sessions and talk about whatever. Let Cat Poop think what he wants.

Like today. He wanted to talk about friends.

"Do you have any friends?" he asked me.

"Define friends," I said.

"People you enjoy spending time with," he suggested. "People you share things with."

"Do invisible ones count?" I asked. "Because then there's Mr. Binky Funstuff and Giggles the Madcap Elf."

"Let's stick with real ones," said Cat Poop. I think he's getting used to me, because he didn't even push his glasses up or tap his pencil.

"Mr. Binky Funstuff doesn't appreciate being called not real," I said. "He's crying. You should apologize."

Cat Poop scratched his nose but didn't say anything.

"Have it your way," I said after a minute. "Sure, I have friends."

"Tell me about them," said Cat Poop.

"Why?" I asked him. "What do they have to do with anything?"

"I'm just curious," he answered. "I'd like to know what you find important in a friend."

"Cash is always nice," I said. "And an entourage."

"I was thinking more along the lines of personality traits," he said. "The qualities you value in other people."

"Well, cleanliness and godliness are always good," I told him.

"How about honesty?" asked Cat Poop. He totally ignores me now when I'm being sarcastic. I don't know if I should be offended or not.

"Honesty is overrated," I said.

"How so?"

"Well, if you're always honest, then you have to tell your friends *everything*," I said. "And sometimes it's better not to."

"Give me an example," said Cat Poop.

"Say she asks you if her jeans make her look fat," I

said. "And they do. If you tell her that, she's going to hate you."

"Even if it's true?" said Cat Poop.

"Especially if it's true," I told him. "A real friend would lie and say the jeans look great."

He wrote on his pad. "Are you making notes for a self-help book?" I asked him. "Because I have lots of tips."

"So you don't think your friend would want to know that the jeans don't look good?" he asked.

"She already knows they don't," I said. "She just wants me to make her feel better. It's just one of those things you don't tell someone, just like you would never tell your friend you hate her boyfriend. Or girlfriend," I added quickly. "Boyfriend or girlfriend."

"Isn't that being dishonest?" suggested Cat Poop. "What if that person isn't right for your friend? Shouldn't you say so?"

"People always say they want to hear the truth, but they really don't," I said. "Like how many parents really want to know that their kids are having sex or smoking? Even if they ask, they just want you to say that everything's fine. Then they can believe that it is."

"And you think that's healthy?" he asked me.

"You're the shrink," I said. "You tell me."

"I'm interested in hearing what you think," said Cat Poop.

I waited a minute before I answered. "What I think is that the goatee you're trying to grow looks ridiculous," I said.

He looked surprised. Then he glanced at the mirror that hangs on one of the walls.

"See?" I said. "Honesty isn't so great, is it?"

DAY 21

A couple of years ago my dad took us all to Hawaii over spring break. One of the things we did there was learn how to scuba dive. It was sort of fun, even though when we first got in the pool to learn how to use all the gear, I was afraid the air would just run out and I'd drown. But I got used to it.

And let me tell you, there is some far-out stuff under the water. Our instructor said that something like 70 percent of the world is covered by water, and less than 1 percent of the population ever gets to go under there and look around. So when you do, you're seeing stuff that not many people get to see. My favorite was this fish that kept swimming up to my mask and butting his head against it. I had no idea what he was doing, but when we got back to the surface the instructor said the fish was trying to fight his reflection in my mask.

That's how I feel being in this place, like I'm a diver looking at a bunch of really strange fish. Take today. For our group session, Cat Poop (who by the way shaved off the goatee, so that's another point for me) had us do this completely retarded exercise. First he split us into two teams. Again, I ended up with Juliet, which left Sadie with Rankin. Martha got to be the audience, since she still isn't exactly talking a blue streak. Then we had to pick these slips of paper out of three different boxes. The first one was a setting, the second was a situation, and the third was a line of dialogue.

The idea was that we had to come up with a skit using the three different things. We had ten minutes to come up with something, and then we had to perform it. I let Juliet pick the slips. Our setting was a theater, our situation was that someone had forgotten something, and our line of dialogue was, "Would you like another cookie?" When we looked at what we had, we both groaned. I mean, come on, what are you supposed to do with that? But that's the whole point of the exercise, right? So we went off in a corner and threw some ideas around.

Juliet is the one who came up with the idea for the husband forgetting his wife's name. Brilliant. It totally worked. I was the husband, and Juliet was my wife. The idea was that we run into someone I work with during intermission at a play and I'm trying to introduce my wife, but for some reason I can't remember her name.

I decided to use Martha for the third person, since she wouldn't have to say anything. She stood there and Juliet and I pretended to run into her. I kept saying things about how great the show was, trying to avoid introducing my wife to Martha, and the whole time Juliet was pretending to eat these cookies she had in her purse. That was how we got the line of dialogue in: Juliet kept offering me cookies.

Okay, so you kind of had to be there. Trust me, it was good. At least *we* thought it was.

Sadie and Rankin's skit was better than ours, but in our defense I have to say it's because they got way better things to work with. Their setting was a spaceship, their situation was that they were lost, and their line was, "How did that get in here?"

The two of them sat in side-by-side chairs, like

they were piloting a spaceship. Sadie was the captain and Rankin was a brand new navigator on his first trip into space. He had managed to get them lost, and was arguing about it with the captain. While they were fighting, a fly was buzzing around, making everything worse. That's when Rankin's character said, "How did that get in here?" and opened a window in the ship to shoo the fly out. Because they were in space, they both got sucked out the window along with the fly, which the two of them acted out by rolling around on the floor together and screaming.

See what I mean about watching a lot of weird fish? Sometimes they look normal, but then one day they go and do something that totally surprises you— and it gets them landed in a place like this. I don't think anyone who knows me would ever have thought I'd do what I did.

But I did.

DAY 22

It was the "Fun with Marjorie and Eric Show" again today. Otherwise known as my parents' weekly visit. Seeing them wasn't high on my list of preferred activities for today, but I didn't have much choice. It was that or, well, nothing.

The theme of today's get together was Why? As in, *Why did Jeff do what he did*? Again, not really something I felt like discussing, but it wasn't up to me.

Apparently Cat Poop had talked to my parents before I came in, because the three of them seemed to have some kind of plan for getting me to talk about what happened. First, Cat Poop told my parents how well things had been going with me. Then he asked my parents to tell me how they'd felt when they found me that night.

My mother immediately turned on the water-works. She said she'd come upstairs and seen blood all over the floor. She said at first she'd thought I was playing a practical joke on her, and she'd laughed even though she thought it was a mean thing to do. When I didn't respond, she apparently totally freaked out, because my father heard her screaming and ran up to see what was wrong.

I'm not saying she was lying or anything, but I do want to point out that she's always said that if she hadn't become a lawyer, she would have been an actress. Seriously. A couple of years ago she even per-formed in this completely tragic community theater production of *Fiddler on the Roof*. She was actually pretty good, which is why I wouldn't put it past her to make things sound more awful than they really were. I mean, finding your kid almost dead is bound to ruin your night, I get that. But it's like she was trying to make me feel even worse about it.

My father didn't cry, but he said that seeing me on the floor like that was the most horrible thing that's ever happened to him. Then he described how he'd made these tourniquets using some torn-up sheets from my bed and held me until the paramedics got there. He said he kept telling me how much he loved me, over and over, in case hearing it helped me stay alive.

That got to me way more than my mother crying. My dad never says sappy stuff to us. He's the kind of guy who can sit through a movie that has everyone else bawling like babies and all he'll say is, "Can you believe how big Julia Roberts's mouth is?" I'm serious. Nothing gets to him. He's like one of those cowboys in an old western.

Listening to my parents talk about that night, I thought about the time Sadie asked me who had saved me. She was right that it was my mom and dad and not the paramedics. If my mother hadn't come up to see me, and if my dad hadn't known what to do, I really would have died. Three weeks ago, that's what I thought I wanted. Now things seem different. Not totally different, but different enough that I guess I'm glad they did what they did. But I wasn't about to tell them that.

Then Cat Poop asked me how I felt about what my parents had said. What are you supposed to say to something like that? Gee, I'm really sorry I freaked you out, and thanks for making sure it didn't work out?

147

It just sounds so stupid, like the big moment in one of those cheesy made-for-TV movies where the kid who ran away from home and became a hooker does a giant boo-hoo after her mother fights off her pimp with an umbrella to get her off the street. I couldn't say those things, even if I *was* thankful for what they did. And I was. I mean I am. Thankful. Sort of. On good days.

What I did say was that I was sorry for making them worry. That seemed like a good compromise, right in between the stony, uncommunicative teenager and the cry-till-your-nose-runs breakdown I could have gone with. I said I was sorry that they were afraid for me and reassured them that everything was okay now.

I should have left out that last part about everything being okay now, because that's one of those statements the doc jumps on like a cat on a mouse.

Sure enough, he said, "What's different about how you are today from how you were that night?"

Oh, man. He pushed me right into that one. Here we were back at the big Why? I was supposed to show how much I'd learned about myself, and they were supposed to get some answer to explain it all. But like I keep saying, there is no big reason.

I had to say something, though, so I said, "I guess

I've learned that no matter how bad things get, there are always people who love you."

I won't blame you if you stop to go throw up right about now. I know I would. But it sounds pretty good, right? If you were my parents, you'd buy it. And they did. I felt a little bad when I saw the look on my mother's face. She seemed really relieved, like she'd been worried all along that the reason I tried to off myself was because I thought she didn't love me. But that was never it. I know she and my father love me. This was never about them.

I think Cat Poop knew I was handing them a big pile of crap and calling it a present, because he pushed me even further and said, "How would you handle things differently now, Jeff?"

What I wanted to say was, "I'd lock my door." I was getting tired of having to make everyone feel better. I'm sorry I freaked everyone out. I'm sorry my parents are sad about it. But it's over. Can we all move on?

I thought for a minute or two until I wasn't quite so steamed, then I said, "I'd talk to somebody." I didn't say *who*. I just said I would talk to somebody. That way they could each think I meant them.

It was the right answer, I guess, because Cat Poop finished with the third degree and moved on to some other stuff. It wasn't anything exciting, so I won't go into it. Basically, he talked to us about better ways to communicate. Blah. Blah. Blah.

I was really thrilled when it was all over and my parents went home. I was even more thrilled to go back to my room. Let me tell you, writing a report on *Lord of the Flies*, which is what I was doing for my English class assignment, is way better than spending an hour with the doc and my parents. Given a choice between discussing the symbolism of a pig head on a stick and discussing my feelings, I'll take the pig head every time.

Day 23

Something totally weird just happened. I'm not even sure I want to write about it, but if I don't I'm afraid it will just stay in my head, and I don't want it in there.

It's about three in the morning. I woke up a while ago and had to pee, so I walked down to the bathroom at the end of the hall. The guys' bathroom here is like the ones at school: sinks and toilets and showers all in one big room. When I walked in, I heard one of the showers running. That was kind of strange, because people mostly shower in the morning, and we're really not supposed to be running around at night except if we have to, you know, go.

Still, it wasn't really a big deal. I mean, we're all in

here because we're a little bit off in the first place, so someone deciding to shower in the middle of the night is pretty tame on the scale of things. So I started to pee, and that's when I heard it. And by *it* I mean this groaning sound.

I made myself stop peeing—which is really, really hard to do when you have to go, by the way—and listened, thinking that maybe I'd just heard noises in the pipes or something. But there it was again, definitely human, and definitely coming from the shower. Now, besides me the only guy here is Rankin, so I knew it had to be him, unless one of the night attendants had suddenly decided to practice some personal hygiene. And judging from the noise, Rankin wasn't feeling too well.

I wasn't sure if I should ask if he was okay or just leave him alone. Then the groaning got a little louder. My bladder was about to pop, so I finished peeing and walked toward the shower. I didn't want to scare Rankin, so I didn't say anything. If you're taking a shower in the middle of the night and not feeling too well, the last thing you need is someone pulling a *Psycho* and yanking the curtain open.

The thing about those curtains is, they don't really cover the opening to the shower totally. There are gaps on either side, almost like the steam from the showers has made the curtains shrink. It's not like you're flashing the whole world when you take a shower, but you can definitely see around them.

What I saw through the crack was definitely Rankin. Too much of him, actually. I didn't mean to, but what I saw was his hand moving back and forth somewhere around his waist, if you know what I mean. Even with all that steam, it was pretty obvious what was going on. Suddenly the groaning made sense.

I wanted to turn around and get out of there, but I couldn't. I was afraid if I did anything, he'd hear me and think I was spying on him. Even my heart beating sounded like a drum banging away inside my chest. I just stood there, watching him but trying not to, and thinking of any way to get out of the bathroom.

It isn't like I've never seen a guy with a hard-on before. Sometimes a guy in gym class will get one in the showers, and everyone points and makes fun of him and calls him a fag, but we all know it's just what happens to guys. We can't help it. It's like that thing is just *there* and it does whatever it wants. It totally is out of our control.

And it's not like I've never jacked off. I'm fifteen years old. Of course I do it. Any guy who says he doesn't is lying. That would be like having the coolest video game ever and never playing it. No one's that stupid.

But I've never seen someone else doing it. It's one of those things you don't really think about other people doing, probably because if you did, every time someone shook your hand you'd be thinking about what else it had been holding on to. You just don't go there.

Only now I *was* there, live and in person. Not two feet away from me, Rankin was going at it like he was all alone in his bedroom with the door locked and the stereo on so no one would hear him. I could hear him getting more and more excited, and I knew what was going to happen. I could partly see his face. His eyes were closed, his mouth was sort of open, and he was breathing hard. Then he sort of grimaced, and I knew it was time to get out of there, while he was still riding high and probably wouldn't notice if a train crashed through the wall of the bathroom.

I waited too long. I was about to turn and get out when he opened his eyes. He looked right at me. At first he just blinked a couple of times, like he thought maybe he was seeing things and needed to clear his head. Then he realized I was real, and he gave me this half smile and nodded, like we were just passing in the hallway. "Hey," he said.

I nodded back. "Hey," I said. *Hey*, like that. What an idiot. Rankin didn't say anything else, so I turned and left.

I don't know what I expected him to do. I don't know what *I* would do if someone caught me spanking the monkey like that. Probably I'd drop dead. I know I wouldn't just say, "Hey."

And now I can't get the image of Rankin out of my head. That's the worst part. I keep picturing his hand going up and down and hearing that groaning. I feel like such a queer. I have to stop thinking about it.

Why did I have to go in there? Why did I have to see that? I can't tell you how much I did *not* need to see that tonight. Or any night.

Maybe I shouldn't make such a big deal out of it. It's not like Rankin seems to care, so why should I? I should just try to forget it ever happened. That's what I'll do. I'll go to bed and forget about it.

DAY 24

You know how Hindus believe that when you die you come back as something or someone else, and that if you screw up the life you have now you come back as something worse until you learn your lesson? Well, if that's true, then I must have really pissed off God—or whoever—in my last life. Otherwise what happened today would never have happened. It's even worse than what happened last night.

See, I'd done an okay job of forgetting what I'd seen Rankin doing in the shower. Even at breakfast, while he choked down his oatmeal, I could sort of pretend I'd just dreamed it. Then we had group. And that's when Cat Poop announced that we were going to do some more pairing off. As soon as he said it, I felt my stomach knot up. I closed my eyes and waited to hear him say I could pair with Sadie or even Juliet.

But of course you know what happened. And it gets even worse, if that's possible. The exercise we did involved picking questions out of a box. There were all of these strips of paper in there, and each one had a question on it. Things like "What are you most proud of in your life?" and "If you could change one thing about yourself, what would it be?"

We were supposed to pick a question and talk about it with our partner. I really, really hoped I got something easy, like "What is the meaning of life in three words or less?" What I actually got was "What's the most embarrassing thing that's ever happened to you?"

I know. I swear to God, that was the question. Sometimes I think there's someone up there just sitting around thinking of ways to make me look like a complete moron. Seriously, I bet there's an angel—or, more likely, a demon—assigned just to me. And every day it gets up and asks itself what it can do to ruin my life. Well, today it got an A plus.

So Rankin and I pair off. I'm still not really looking at him, just sort of *around* him. And of course all I can picture is that big hand of his going up and down, and then I'm staring at his crotch remembering what's *there*, and eventually the only place I can look is at his face, and when I do I'm surprised to see that he doesn't seem the least bit embarrassed.

Instead, he's looking at the paper in his hand. He's looking really hard, like he can't quite figure out what it says, like it's written in Japanese or something. He looks and looks and looks, and finally he looks at me and says, "What do you think about when you jerk off?"

I know you think I'm making this up, but I swear I'm not. That's exactly what he said. I sat there staring at Rankin, sure I'd heard him wrong. Then this big grin spreads across his face, and he starts to laugh.

"Got you," he said.

I wanted to hit him, I really did. I couldn't believe he did that. He thought it was hysterical, though. He was grinning his big stupid jock grin from ear to ear and rocking back and forth with laughter.

"Would you shut up!" I said.

Rankin wiped his eyes and quieted down. "I'm sorry," he said. "But you should see the look on your face."

"What does it really say?" I asked him.

"Why?" he said. "Don't you want to know the answer to the question I read?"

"Not really," I told him.

"All right," he said. He looked at the paper again and read the right question. "What's the hardest thing you've ever done?"

He sighed. "I guess that would be telling my dad that I don't want to play football anymore."

"I thought you liked to play football."

"I do. I just don't want to play on the team anymore."

"Why not?" I asked him.

Rankin shook his head. "I just don't," he said. "What's your question say?"

"Just a minute," I told him. "You can't say you 'just don't want to.' We're supposed to talk about this crap. I want to know why you don't want to be Mr. Big Football Player."

Rankin put his head down. For a second I thought he was going to tackle me, but he just sat there. When he looked up, I could see he was trying really hard not to cry.

"Do you know what it's like to have everyone expect you to be the best at something?" he said.

I shook my head. "That's not a problem for me," I

told him. "I'm not good at anything. Nothing important, anyway."

"I am," Rankin said. "I'm good at throwing a ball and catching a ball and knocking people out of the way when they get between me and the ball. That's what I'm good at."

"So what's the problem with that? Everybody loves jocks, right?" I admit I said it kind of sarcastically, because he sounded like such a bonehead and I was still mad at him about what he'd done before.

"Yeah," Rankin said, snorting. "Everybody loves you. When you win. Then you're the hero. But when you lose, you're just the stupid meathead who couldn't make the play."

I was having a hard time feeling sorry for the guy. I know that sounds harsh. But I wasn't ready to let him off the hook for being a jock in the first place. Everybody knows those guys get most of the breaks in school, and it seems to me that if all they have to worry about is playing a dumb game, then they have it pretty easy.

"You know what my father said when I told him I wanted to quit?" Rankin asked me.

"I wasn't there," I said. "You'll have to fill me in."

"He said if I wasn't going to play football, I wasn't his son."

"He did not," I said. "Why would he say something so stupid?"

"Because it's how he feels," said Rankin. "That's all he sees me as, a football player. He was a football player. His dad was a football player. *His* dad was a football player. That's what the guys in my family are."

"But you're his kid," I said, still not believing him.

"And as far as he's concerned, his kid plays football." He laughed. "Why do you think I'm here?"

"Because you get down sometimes," I said, remembering what he'd said the first time in group.

"Yeah," said Rankin. "But that's not the real reason I'm here."

"Then why'd you say that?" I asked him.

"Come on. Nobody says why they're really here," Rankin answered. "Not at first. Nobody wants to be the biggest freak. Didn't you?"

"Didn't I what?"

"Lie," he said.

"It's kind of hard to when you've got these," I said, showing him my wrists.

"But that doesn't say *why*," he reminded me.

"So we both lied," I said. "Why are you really here?"

"Because my father wants to know what's wrong with me."

"He sent you to the psych ward because you don't want to play football? You've got to be kidding."

"I'm not," said Rankin. "That's why I'm here."

"That's messed up," I told him. "Supremely messed up."

Rankin nodded. "Yeah, it is. So what's your question?"

I told him. "And I think you know the answer to that one already," I added, knowing I was probably turning a hundred different shades of red.

"Your wrists," he said.

I looked at him. Did he really not get it? *No, not my wrists*, I wanted to say. *It was walking in on you pulling your pork*.

Rankin either didn't think that was embarrassing, or he was trying to pretend it never happened. But I don't think that was it. I think he honestly didn't think it was a big deal.

I would. Seriously, I'd rather have someone walk in on me cutting my wrists than have them see me doing that. Between you and me, I think Rankin's priorities are a little screwed up.

Day 25

I told Sadie. About seeing Rankin in the shower. I wasn't going to, but I couldn't stop thinking about it, and I thought maybe if I told someone, I'd get it out of my head and into someone else's. You know, like that movie *The Ring*, where the characters have to pass along the haunted videotape to someone else so that the ghost girl in the video won't come out and kill them. They know the girl will kill the person they give the tape to, but they do it anyway because they don't want to die more than they don't want to be responsible for someone else dying.

Not that picturing Rankin would kill me, but it *was* giving me a pretty bad headache. So bad that I

163

couldn't sleep. I went into the lounge, and there was Sadie. I don't think she ever sleeps. I think she just watches TV all night.

"It was so weird," I said after I told her the basics.

"Why?" she asked me.

"What do you mean *why*?" I asked back. "Because it's weird."

"Please," she said. "Like you don't do it too."

I almost said I didn't, but that would have been an obvious lie. I mean, come on. I bet even the Pope does it.

"But he wasn't even embarrassed," I said.

"Is it big?" asked Sadie.

"Is what big?" I said.

"You know," Sadie said, looking down with her eyes. "*It*. He's a big guy. I bet it's big."

"I didn't exactly notice," I told her.

She grinned. "Yes, you did," she said.

"I did not!" I protested.

She rolled her eyes. "You know you did," she said. "Guys always look. They have to compare. So, is he bigger than you?"

"You are such a perv," I said.

"What is it with guys?" she asked me. "Girls always compare."

"Big deal," I said. "It's not as if there's a lot of difference between . . ." This time it was my turn to look down in the general area of her, you know, girl parts.

"How do you know?" she shot back. "How many of them have you seen?"

"Enough," I said.

"Like Allie's?" Sadie asked, surprising me.

I felt myself turning red, which totally made me mad. "All right," I said. "So I saw it. I guess it was pretty big. Are you happy?"

"Are we talking about Allie or Rankin now?" said Sadie, grinning again.

"I should never have brought this up," I said.

"Relax," Sadie said. "Let's get back to the problem. Why are you so freaked out about this?"

"What if . . ." I started.

"What if what?" asked Sadie when I didn't finish.

I took a deep breath. "What if he *wanted* me to see him?" I said.

Sadie laughed. "So what if he did?"

"That's kind of creepy," I said.

"Please, it wasn't like he asked you to help out or something," she said. "You just wandered in."

"But he didn't seem to *care* that I saw him," I said.

"Why should he?" Sadie asked. "It's no big deal.

You guys are always walking around with those things sticking out and touching yourselves and whatever. It's like you're so proud of them that you have to show them off."

"Sure," I said. "It's like a dog show. Sometimes we even have talent contests."

Sadie shook her head. "Guys are so fucked up. You get all freaked out about people thinking you're gay if you look at each other. Girls aren't so hung up about that."

"What do you mean?" I asked her.

"Well," she said. "Have you ever practiced making out with one of your guy friends?"

"No!" I said.

"See," said Sadie. "But girls do it all the time."

"You do?"

"Sure. I've made out with lots of my friends. Sometimes more than that."

"More how?" I asked her.

"You know, a little touching and stuff. No major lesbo action or anything. Not that there's anything wrong with that. I mean, I'd probably do that with the right girl."

I didn't know what to say. To be honest, she was freaking me out a little bit.

166

"I don't think guys do that kind of stuff," I said.

She laughed. "You just don't admit that you do," she said. "Trust me. Guys do it, too."

I don't know about that. I can't imagine many of the guys at my school playing around with each other during a sleepover. But maybe they do. They sure slap each other's butts enough in the locker room and on the field. I always thought that was weird, by the way. Guys are so afraid of people thinking they're queer, but the jocks are practically feeling each other up out there.

I didn't want to think about it anymore, so I changed the subject. Actually, I suggested that we play the dialogue game. I figured that might distract Sadie from the whole sex subject.

It didn't. As soon as we started playing, I knew I was in trouble. The movie was one of those really bad teen slasher movies. It took place at a summer camp (don't they all?), where someone was offing all of the counselors for no apparent reason.

The scene we were watching was about two of the counselors, a guy and a girl. For some reason that would only make sense in a bad teen slasher movie, they had decided to go camping in the woods when there were perfectly good cabins right there. They were inside a tent, sort of half in and half out of their sleeping bags, and they were talking. It was perfect for the dialogue game.

"Let's do something different," Sadie suggested. "I'll be the guy. You be the girl."

She didn't wait for me to say okay; she just started in. "Heather, there's no one in the woods."

"But I heard something, Sean," I said as the girl moved her mouth.

Sean put his hand on Heather's cheek. "It's just the wind," Sadie said.

The girl looked like she didn't believe him. "I'd feel better if I was in your sleeping bag with you," I said in her voice.

As Sean unzipped his sleeping bag and the girl in the movie slid out of hers, Sadie said, "I hope you don't mind, but I sleep in the nude."

"Oh," I said, trying to sound like a girl who was surprised. "I wish I'd shaved my legs."

"That's okay," Sadie replied in a low voice. "I like a girl with hairy legs. It turns me on."

We both laughed. Then I did something I hadn't planned on. I slid my hand over and put it on top of Sadie's. My heart was fluttering like a crazy butterfly, and for a second I almost pulled my hand back. But then Sadie folded her fingers around mine. She didn't say anything or even look at me. It was like she'd expected me to do it.

We sat like that while we kept playing the game.

"You're so warm," I said in Heather's voice.

"That's because you make me warm," said Sadie.

"Oh, Sean," I said. "I feel so safe with you."

"Safe enough to go all the way?" said Sadie.

I hesitated along with the girl in the movie. When she started moving her lips again I said, "I think so."

Just at that moment, a knife plunged through the tent wall. The guy and the girl screamed and tried to get away as the killer came at them, but they were tangled in the sleeping bag. The knife came down again and again, and blood went everywhere.

"So much for Heather's first time," Sadie said in her normal voice. "She died a virgin. How sad."

She was still holding my hand. But now that we weren't playing the game, it felt a little strange. Still, neither of us let go of the other's hand. I kind of felt like I should say or do something, but I didn't know what.

We sat like that until the movie was over. I can't even tell you how it ended. All I could think about was how warm Sadie's hand was, and how I hoped I wasn't sweating or anything. I forgot all about Rankin and, well, everything. It was like when I touched her, some magnetic force in her hand erased all of the stuff in my head.

"All right you two, I think that's enough television for tonight."

Nurse Moon's voice startled me. I'd forgotten all about her. For a minute it was like Sadie and I were just sitting in the living room at home. But Moonie's voice reminded me where we really were.

It also reminded me that Sadie and I weren't supposed to be holding hands. I let go of hers just as Nurse Moon walked over and clicked the TV off.

"Off to bed," she said.

I mumbled a good night to Sadie without looking at her, then walked back to my room. As I was going in, I heard Sadie whisper, "Hey."

I turned around. She glanced back at the lounge, then leaned in and kissed me quick on the lips. "Good night," she said.

Day 26

Oh, man. Cat Poop *cannot* find out about this. *Nobody* can find out about this. If they do, Sadie and I are both screwed.

Okay, so after Sadie kissed me good night last night, she went back to her room. Nothing else happened. But the thing is, I kept wondering what *could* have happened. And the more I thought about it, the more I wished something *had* happened. I tried not to picture it, but when I tried focusing on something else, I kept seeing Rankin again. I definitely didn't want to go there, so I switched back to Sadie.

That's when I got up. I told myself I was just going to go to the bathroom. And I did go. I went in there

171

and peed. I thought about taking a shower to relax, but shower = Rankin, and that was *not* helping. So I started to go back to my room.

But when I walked into the hallway, I ran into Carl. I haven't mentioned him before because he wasn't important before, but now he's *really* important. Carl walks through the halls every half hour to make sure no one is doing anything they shouldn't be doing. He's not an attendant, exactly, because he doesn't help the nurses with anything medical. He's more of a night watchman.

Actually, there are two watchmen, and they alternate nights. The other one is a guy named Frank. Frank's not very friendly. He just does his rounds and almost never says anything. Honestly, I don't think he'd care if he found one of us dead on the floor. He'd just keep going.

But Carl is different. Carl's a nice guy. He's got to be at least sixty. He reminds me of my grandfather. Actually, he *is* a grandfather. I know because he's shown me pictures of his grandkids. You always know when Carl's around because his keys jangle when he walks, like he's kind of bouncing and the keys knock against his leg. You'd think it would be totally distracting, but it's actually kind of reassuring to hear him walking past my room.

"Hey, sport," Carl said when he saw me. He calls everybody sport. It must be a grandpa thing, because mine does it, too. "Can't sleep?" he asked.

"Uh, just had to, you know, pee," I told Carl.

He jangled his keys. "I know how that is," he said. "The older you get, the more you go. I must go four times a night. I've got a bladder like a leaky roof."

"Right," I said. I mean, what do you say when someone tells you about their bladder? *Gee, maybe you should wear a diaper?*

"Well, you get back to bed," said Carl. "I'm heading over to see the other folks for a while."

He meant he was heading over to the adult ward. Carl always talks about the patients as if they're his next-door neighbors. I guess he doesn't want to make us feel bad about being here; unlike Frank, who I once heard whistling the theme music from the Looney Tunes cartoon show while he was making his rounds.

"See you, sport," Carl said as he walked away.

"See you," I said back.

I started to go to my room, but something made me turn around. I looked down the hall to where the girls' rooms are. Carl had just walked through, and I knew he wouldn't be back for at least half an hour. As long as

Moonie stayed in the nurses' station, I would have thirty minutes before anyone checked on me.

I moved before I could stop myself. I was at Sadie's door in about ten seconds, and inside right after that. Then I went to her bed. She was asleep on her back. Her hands were on her stomach, and her hair was all over the pillow. Her mouth was open, but she wasn't snoring or anything. She was just asleep.

I leaned down and kissed her, just like in the movies. When I pulled my head back, her eyes were open and she was looking at me with this dreamy expression.

"Hey," she said, all sleepy.

"Hey," I said. "Mind if I share your sleeping bag?"

She didn't say anything, but she scooted over and lifted the blanket and sheet. I got in next to her.

"Carl will be back in half an hour," I said.

Honestly, until right then I hadn't known I was going to do what I did next. I reached out and I put my hand on Sadie's breast. She was wearing a T-shirt, but I felt everything.

I wasn't sure what to do next. Then Sadie put her hand on mine, like she had when we were sitting on the couch. "It's okay," she said, still sounding half asleep. "You can pretend I'm Allie."

She took my hand and slid it under her T-shirt. Her nipple poked into my palm, and the skin was warm. I squeezed. Sadie made this funny little noise, like a sigh and a groan all at once. Then she took my hand and moved it down to her panties. I felt the elastic waistband and stopped there. My heart was beating so hard I was sure she could feel it.

"It's okay," she said again.

I slipped my fingers underneath the elastic and felt hair. I don't know why, but I was surprised that it was as rough as mine is. I thought girls would have really soft hair down there, like rabbit fur or something. It felt strange. Also, I'm used to feeling, well, *something* down there, and it wasn't there.

Sadie made a soft grunting sound and kissed my neck. I could feel myself getting hard, but I didn't know what to do next. Was I just supposed to stick it in? Was there something else I was supposed to do first? In the movies they always end the scene before you see that part. And it's not like someone gives you a manual or anything. I just figured that when the time came, I'd know what to do. But there I was, and I had no clue.

Sadie put her hand into my boxers. I pulled away from her and rolled onto my side.

"What's wrong?" she asked.

"I hear Carl," I said. "His keys."

"I didn't hear anything," Sadie said. "It's probably just the wind." She started to touch me again, but I wasn't hard anymore.

"I'm sorry," I said. "I should go."

I didn't wait for her to say anything else. I just left. Of course, Carl wasn't in the hall. I knew he wasn't. I ran back to my room as fast as I could and got into my own bed.

Day 27

I knew I couldn't avoid Sadie forever. I mean, it's not like there's, oh, *anywhere* to get away from people for very long around here. In fact, I pretty much ran into her first thing at breakfast.

"Hey," I said, which is so incredibly witty that you can applaud my genius any time you want to.

"Hey," Sadie said. "Take my advice, stay away from the muffins. They look like blueberries, but they're actually raisins. Totally disgusting."

She was talking like it was any other day and not the morning after I tried to have sex with her but couldn't keep it up. I figured she was just being nice and pretending it hadn't happened.

"I'm sorry about what happened," I said. Lucky for me, no one else had come in yet, so I didn't have to worry about anyone eavesdropping. Well, except for anyone listening on the hidden microphones, which by the way I totally believe are planted around here.

"What about it?" Sadie asked, poking at her oatmeal with her spoon.

"You know," I said, not believing she was going to make me actually say it. "Not being able to—"

"Oh, that," said Sadie, waving her hand like she was shooing away a fly. "Don't worry about it. We were just fooling around, right? It's not like it was our honeymoon."

"I just wanted you to know that it wasn't because of, you know, you or anything."

"Oh, I know," Sadie answered. "I never thought it was. It's all about you."

"Gee, thanks," I said. I felt like she'd slapped me.

"No," she said, looking at my face. "I didn't mean it that way. I mean I know it's because of you. You and Allie."

"Me and Allie?" I repeated.

"Sure," Sadie said. "You're in love with her and she doesn't love you. Or something like that. I still haven't quite figured it all out. But I know it's about Allie."

"It's not like that," I said, shaking my head. "She's just my best friend."

"Best friend," Sadie repeated, making air quotes with her fingers so that I would know she didn't really believe me. "Okay, so you and Allie are best friends. That doesn't mean you don't want to be more than that. So what's the problem?"

"It's not a problem," I said. "Or at least it wasn't. Not until Burke came into the picture."

"Who's Burke?"

"Allie's boyfriend." It was the first time I'd said his name out loud since coming to the hospital. It tasted like raw onions.

Sadie nodded. "I get it now. You're jealous because Burke's got Allie, and Burke's all jealous because you and Allie are friends. That is *such* a guy thing. He probably gets all pissed off because he thinks she spends more time with you than with him."

"Right," I said.

"And because she's a girl and thinks boyfriends are the most important thing in the universe, she told you she couldn't spend so much time with you."

"Something like that." Sort of.

"God, girls make me sick sometimes," said Sadie. "Here's this jerk who'll probably dump her in a month and she gives up her best friend for him because he's too insecure to handle the fact that she likes to hang out with another guy. What a stupid bitch."

I didn't say anything. Allie isn't stupid, and she isn't a bitch. If she was, what happened between us would be easier to forget. But she's not like that at all, only I couldn't tell Sadie that because it would make her think I wasn't telling the whole story. Which I wasn't.

"That's why you did it, isn't it?" Sadie said after a minute. "Because you lost your best friend?"

"Pretty much," I said. "I don't know, maybe I thought it would make her feel sorry for me or something. Pretty stupid, huh?"

"Not stupid," said Sadie. "Sad. Especially because she doesn't deserve a friend like you."

Then she got up and hugged me. I totally wasn't expecting it. Like I said before, my family isn't big on the whole affection thing. I mean Amanda hugged me when she saw me, but that was just a case of temporary insanity. Normally she would never do that. Even Allie has never hugged me more than a couple of times, and she comes from a big family of huggers. I guess I just have this invisible sign on me that says NO HUGGING.

But Sadie ignored the sign. She hugged me really

hard, patting my back and squeezing me. I wasn't sure what I should do, so I patted her back. That seemed to work, because she let go of me.

"I'm so sorry that happened to you," she said. "But you know what? You don't need her. It's time you had friends who see how great you are."

"Maybe," I said.

"No maybe," said Sadie, taking my hands and holding them. Her thumbs touched my wrists, and I could feel her rubbing my scars. I let her.

"I want you to know you can tell me anything," Sadie said. "*Anything.*"

"Thanks," I told her. "You too."

"Aren't you two a cute couple."

I looked up and saw Rankin grinning at us. He was carrying a plate piled with scrambled eggs, sausage, toast, and everything else he could fit on it. I don't think I could eat that much food in an entire day, let alone for breakfast.

Rankin took a seat at the table while Sadie went back to her chair. To tell the truth, I was kind of relieved that Rankin had interrupted us. I mean, I was happy that Sadie wasn't mad, and it was nice of her to say everything she said, but I had pretty much used up all of my sharing time minutes, if you know what I mean.

Rankin was ignoring us and concentrating on his breakfast. And I mean *concentrating*, as in he was staring at it like it was a math problem he needed to figure out. Finally he picked up a sausage and bit one end off.

"Take it easy on that thing, Rankin," said Sadie, looking at me and winking. "You know what they say about playing with your sausage too much."

I couldn't believe she'd said that. "*Stop it*," I mouthed at her.

But it didn't matter. Rankin didn't get the joke, anyway. He wrinkled up his eyebrows and said, "I'm not playing with it, I'm eating it." He put the rest of the sausage in his mouth and chewed it.

Sadie looked at me and giggled.

"You guys are weird," Rankin said, and dug into his eggs.

Day 28

What happened tonight wasn't a dream. I want it to be, but it wasn't. It really happened. And now I feel worse than I did when they took me off the happy pill that first week. A lot worse. I almost feel the way I did the night I tried to, well, do what I did.

I went to bed around eleven last night. Even though things were okay between us, I was still a little freaked out about what happened with Sadie, and I just wanted to sleep for a while and forget about it. You know how things always seem worse at night, and how in the morning they aren't that bad? Well, that's not *always* true. Not this time, anyway.

I *was* dreaming. In my dream I was running along

a street somewhere. It was nighttime, and the moon was full. The stars were all silver and shining, and it was warm, the perfect summer night. I was just running along. Then I spread my arms, like you do when you're a kid and you're pretending to be an airplane, and the wind lifted me into the sky.

There I was, flying. It's not like I've never had a flying dream before, but this was different. I felt like a kite, riding the wind and watching the town below me. It looked like a miniature city, all the lights twinkling and the cars moving around like fireflies. It was totally beautiful and peaceful, and I never wanted it to end.

Then something happened. It was like the dream skipped a few frames, or someone hit the pause button in my brain. In my dream I started to fall back to earth. I woke up, and for a minute I thought I really had fallen. I didn't know where I was or what was happening.

That's when I realized that someone was in the bed with me. There was a body stretched alongside mine, and the sheets and blankets were pulled back. The moon was shining in through the window, and I could see it reflected on bare skin. Someone was touching me. There was a hand between my legs, stroking me. And I was hard.

"It's okay," a voice whispered in my ear. For a

second, I thought it was Sadie, and that this time I might be able to go through with it.

But it wasn't Sadie. It was Rankin. He was in my bed, naked, and he was jacking me off. It was so totally bizarre that for a minute I was sure I was still dreaming. But I felt his skin on mine, and his hand going up and down. I could even feel his breath where he was breathing against my neck.

All I could say was, "What are you doing?"

"Do you like it?" Rankin asked me.

"Don't," I told him. But I couldn't move. It was like I was frozen. For a minute I thought I was still dreaming, that I might wake up and be alone in my bed. I shut my eyes.

Rankin stopped what he was doing and moved his hand up my belly. His fingers were rough, but they still tickled. When he rested his palm on my chest I could feel the calluses he has from playing ball.

"Your heart is beating really fast," he said. He moved his head closer to me and kissed my neck.

I wanted to tell him to stop. I wanted to tell him to get out of my bed and out of my room. But it was like my voice was locked in my throat. I kept swallowing, trying to break through the block that was there, but nothing worked. *Wake up,* I told myself.

Wake up wake up wake up wake up.

"You can touch me if you want to," said Rankin.

My hands were at my sides, my right one pressed against Rankin's stomach where he was lying next to me. I could feel his skin, and the muscle beneath it. He moved closer, and my fingertips touched skin and hair. I was so scared I couldn't move. Mostly I wanted to be anywhere else, but part of me was really curious.

He pushed himself against me. He was hard. I moved my hand, and my fingers wrapped around him. I wasn't sure why I was doing it. Maybe I was afraid of what would happen if I *didn't* do it. I just pretended I was still dreaming.

Rankin's body tensed, then relaxed, and the two of us just stayed there like that for a while. I could feel the blood pumping through him, and I started moving my hand up and down him. He put his hand back between my legs and did the same thing. Neither of us said anything while we did it, but every so often Rankin would brush his lips against my neck. I don't know how long we were there, but it felt like hours. Then I felt Rankin's body stiffen and he groaned. My hand was covered in sticky heat, and he gripped me harder. A few seconds later I was done too.

I didn't know what to do afterward. Rankin sat up

and wiped his hands on his T-shirt, which he'd thrown on the floor. Then he pulled his underwear on and left without saying anything.

When he was gone, I put my hand to my nose. It was still sticky from him. I could smell Rankin on my fingers, a mix of sweat and something else I can't really describe. I wiped my hand on the sheets to get it off, but the smell stayed in my nose, no matter how hard I breathed to clear it out.

I tried to get back to sleep, but I couldn't. Every time I closed my eyes I could feel Rankin touching me, feel his breath on my neck and his skin against mine.

Why did I do that with him? Why did I let him stay?

I don't know why. But I did, and now I feel like crap. Dirty. Worst of all, I have to see my parents today. And I don't even want to think about having to see Rankin later. Maybe he won't say anything and we can pretend it never happened. He's good at that, right? And maybe it *didn't* happen. Maybe it was all a sick dream, and I'll still wake up.

Day 29

I honestly can't tell you much about how things went with my parents this morning. It was fine, I guess. We basically talked about how much we all love each other and how they're looking forward to having me come home in a couple of weeks. I didn't say much, and for once Cat Poop didn't push me. Maybe he could see how tired I was. I'm sure I'll get grilled about it in our session tomorrow.

Anyway, the point is, I'm sort of preoccupied. For obvious reasons, I tried to avoid Rankin, but I ran into him this morning in the bathroom. I seriously have to talk to somebody about getting my own bathroom. This togetherness thing is becoming a problem.

I wasn't even going to take a shower. That's how much I didn't want to see Rankin. But around here if you don't take a shower, someone will accuse you of being depressed again and you'll have to go through the whole "Is anything troubling you today, Jeff?" bullshit. Who needs it? Also, I didn't want to meet my parents smelling like Rankin's dick.

So of course I walked in and there he was. He had his towel wrapped around his waist, and he was standing outside the shower waiting for the water to get hot. The water here takes forever to warm up. I swear they have, like, three old women in the basement boiling water over actual fires. Then the water takes so long to get up here, it's only warmish when it comes out.

"Hey," Rankin said, like nothing weird had happened.

"Hey," I said back, then stood there feeling like an idiot. But what was I supposed to say? *"Thanks for coming over last night? Sorry I didn't have clean sheets on the bed?"* I mean, what?

I was going to turn around and leave, but right then Rankin dropped his towel. Then he looked at me, nodded toward the shower, and stepped in.

I swear I don't know why I did it, but I followed him. It was like someone else had taken control of my body. Rankin had left the curtain open, and before I knew what I was doing, I stepped inside and pulled it closed behind me.

We just stood there for a while under the water. The stalls aren't that big, so we were basically pressed against each other. I was staring at his chest, noticing how hairy he is and trying not to think about anything. Then Rankin kissed me. His lips pressed against mine. He had some beard stubble, and it felt scratchy on my cheek.

Rankin pushed me against the wall. The tiles were cold, and I tried to move away from them, but Rankin was kind of leaning against me. I put my hands on his chest to try and push him back, but as soon as I touched him it was like someone had glued us together. He put his hands on my butt and pulled me closer. He kept kissing me while he pumped himself against me. He was hard, and I reached down and wrapped my fingers around it.

"Suck it," Rankin said.

I wasn't sure I'd heard him right, so I didn't do anything. Then he put his hands on my shoulders and kind of pushed me down so that I was on my knees. The water splashed on my head and ran down my face. I was staring at his dick and his balls and thinking how big they looked close up.

I don't know why I didn't just get up and leave. I could have. It wasn't like he was holding me prisoner. But I couldn't stop staring at his dick. It was just so weird to be kneeling there in the shower in front of another guy. And for some reason I kept thinking, *I wonder what it tastes like?*

I opened my mouth and put it on the tip of his dick. The skin tasted salty and a little sticky. Rankin put his hands on my head and pushed inside me a little, and I started to choke. He pulled back and I breathed in until I felt more relaxed. Then I tried again.

We didn't do it for very long before I heard him moan. My mouth filled with something warm and salty and I realized Rankin was coming. I didn't want to swallow it, so I held it in my mouth until he pulled out. Then I turned and spit it out.

"I have a buddy I do that with sometimes," Rankin said. He had started to soap himself up, and was washing under his arms.

I didn't say anything. I stood up. I kind of thought he might blow me next, but all he said was, "You should probably get in another shower, in case they come in on rounds."

"Right," I said. I opened the curtain and stepped out. The air was cold, and I shivered as I went to the shower beside Rankin's and turned on the water. I didn't even wait for it to warm up. I got in and then tried to stand close to the wall so that the cold water wouldn't hit me. But it did, and it felt like I was trapped in one of those freak summer storms where you're riding along on your bike and then the sky opens up and dumps rain on you, so that you have to wait it out under a tree. Then your T-shirt is soaking wet and all you can think about is getting home and into something dry.

Rankin was humming. I could hear it through the shower wall. It wasn't really a song, more like this weird out-of-tune melody. I listened to him while the water warmed up or maybe just until I got used to it being cold. Something about the song was familiar. Then I realized he was humming "London Bridge," only not quite right. He sounded like a little kid trying to sing something he'd just learned in school.

I soaped up and tried to ignore him. I could still taste him in my mouth. I wished I had some mouthwash, but I didn't, so I just opened my mouth and let the water fill it up. I swished it around and spit, but I could still taste Rankin's dick. It was like when you eat peppers or something and no matter what you drink, you can't get it off your tongue.

After a few minutes he stopped humming and got out. I heard him drying off. Then he left without saying anything, as if nothing weird had happened. Again.

I stood under that water for a long time. For some reason, I couldn't get that stupid "London Bridge" song out of my head. "London Bridge is falling down," I kept hearing. "Falling down. Falling down. London Bridge is falling down, my fair lady."

When I was little, I had a record of that song. I used to play it over and over. Standing in the shower, I started singing the next words. "Take a key and lock her up. Lock her up. Lock her up. Take a key and lock her up, my fair lady."

For some reason, that made me start crying. I just slid down the wall and sat there in that goddamn shower, crying and singing that stupid song, over and over.

Day 30

I think I've figured out what Rankin's brand of crazy is. He's projecting, or whatever they call it when you accuse someone else of being what you are. Personally, I call it being an asshole, but I guess they needed to come up with a name that sounds more official.

This morning I went to the bathroom to pee. I put it off as long as I could. You know, like when—for whatever reason—you don't want to get out of bed, so you lie there hoping the pee will just magically turn to steam or something. But it doesn't, and eventually you can't stand it anymore and have to get up.

I lasted for maybe half an hour. Then it got to the point where I either had to get out of bed or pee *in* it.

Frankly, I was tempted, but I just couldn't do it. I had to get up.

And there was Rankin. I don't know how he always manages to be in the bathroom when I need to use it, but it's starting to freak me out. He's like one of those dogs who can sense when a person is going to have a seizure, only Rankin senses whenever I need to pee.

He was shaving at one of the sinks. I didn't look at him while I went to the urinal, even though he was literally right behind me. For a few seconds I actually expected to feel him come up behind me again, but he stayed put.

After I peed, I went to wash my hands. I figured I should say something, since Rankin seemed a little edgy.

"Hey, about yesterday," I said. "It's no big deal. You don't have to worry. I'm not going to tell anyone about you."

I figured that was kind of big of me, you know, since *he* was the one who got all gay on me. I mean, I didn't start any of it.

"About me?" he said, making that confused face he does when he doesn't understand something. "What about me?"

"About how you're—you know," I said. "About what happened."

He looked like I'd just called him a puppy killer or something. "Me?" he said. "I was going to say that I won't tell anyone about *you*."

I couldn't believe it. He was the one who came into *my* room. He was the one who touched *me*. Not the other way around. When I told him that, he shook his head.

"No way, man," he said. "I'm not like that. I was just fooling around with you. It's not like there are any girls here to do it with or anything. If we weren't in here, it would never have happened."

"There *are* girls here," I said. I was mad, and I wanted to push him a little.

He made a grunting sound. "None I'd go near," he said. "They're all whack-jobs."

"And what are you?" I asked him. "What am I? In case you hadn't noticed, we're all whack-jobs."

"I'm just saying," said Rankin. "It wasn't anything to get bent out of shape about, okay?"

"Yeah," I said, washing my hands for like the sixth time. "Okay. I wasn't going to say anything, anyway."

He smiled a goofy smile. "Me neither," he said. "So we're good?"

I nodded as I turned off the water. Rankin gave me this weird punch in the shoulder, like we'd just scored a goal or something. Then he went back to shaving and I went back to my room. I waited until I was pretty sure he would be out of the bathroom before I went back for my shower.

I still can't believe he thinks I'm the one with the problem. How is that even possible? Okay, so maybe I was the one who did the sucking, but he was the one who wanted it. I didn't. I just did it because he did.

I can't even think about it right now. It makes me too mad. I'll deal with it later. Besides, there's other stuff on my mind. Namely, leaving.

In my session with Cat Poop today, he reminded me that I'm two-thirds of the way through my forty-five days. On the one hand, that makes it seem like time is flying by. On the other, I feel like I've been here for thirty years, not thirty days.

"You didn't seem very excited about leaving when your parents talked about it yesterday," Cat Poop said. "How come?"

I shrugged. I didn't know what to say. Because here's the weird thing: Sometimes I wish I could stay here forever. It's like being in a castle with a moat around it. Sure, it's a castle filled with crazy people, but at least no one can get in unless we let them in. Of course, we can't get out either, but when you think about it, what's so great about being out there? There's too much out there that can hurt you. In here you don't have to worry about it. You just have to worry about being molested by jocks. But like I said, I'm not thinking about that.

Cat Poop tried another question on me. "What do you want your life to be like when you leave here?" he asked me.

I thought about it for a minute. "I want to be so rich that I can buy my own island and live on it all by myself."

You know what he said? "What about music? What about movies?"

"I'll order them online," I said. "Food, too. You can pretty much get anything online. Did you know you can even buy black widow spiders online?"

It's true. Amanda and I looked it up one day when we were talking about how you could kill someone and get away with it. Just hypothetically, of course. I have enough problems without being a psychopath. Or sociopath. Whatever. Anyway, Amanda thought you could get a whole bunch of black widows, put them in a box, and mail it to whoever you wanted to kill. And it turns out, you can. They aren't even that expensive, something like three bucks each.

"Even friends?" Cat Poop said.

"What do you think most people spend their time online doing?" I asked him. "Isn't that the whole point of the internet, that you can pretend to be someone else so that a bunch of other people will like you? Practically every kid in my school has their own website. And believe me, they make themselves sound a lot more interesting than they really are. Seriously, does Jamie Kazinsky really think anyone is going to believe the pictures her cousin took with his digital camera were used in the Venezuelan edition of *Seventeen*?"

"What about love?" Cat Poop asked me, not answering my question. I'm getting kind of tired of him doing that. Personally, I think it's rude.

"What about it?" I asked back.

"If you're all alone on the island, you won't have anyone there who loves you," he said.

"I think I'll survive somehow," I told him.

"Don't you ever want to be in love?" he said.

I knew where he was going with that. Allie again. Man, he doesn't give up. I guess he thinks one of these days I won't realize what he's doing and spill the beans. Here's a clue, Cat Poop: There are no beans.

"What's love, anyway?" I said. "I think it's just something greeting-card makers made up and try to get us to believe in. Between you and me, I'd rather have an Xbox."

Thankfully, my time was up right about then, and I escaped back to the ward, where it's mostly safe. Rankin being the exception. But I haven't seen him. He's probably in his room reading *Sports Illustrated* and not being gay.

Later on I told Sadie about my session with Cat Poop. "What's his obsession with love?" I asked her.

"I don't know," Sadie said. "But I think love is really important."

I thought for a minute that she was messing with me. Then she looked around, like she was making sure no one was listening, and whispered, "Want to see something?"

She didn't wait for me to answer. Instead, she dug around in her pocket and pulled something out. It was a piece of paper. She unfolded it and handed it to me.

It was a newspaper clipping. The headline was HERO RESCUES GIRL FROM WATERY GRAVE. I looked at Sadie. "This is about you," I said.

She nodded. "Yeah," she said. "I cut it out and kept

it. I have a lot more at home. Sort of a suicide scrap-book. But this one's my favorite."

Alongside the article was a picture of a man. He had a round, happy face and bright blue eyes. He was going bald, and he had a thick moustache.

"That's Sam," Sadie said, seeing me looking at the picture.

"The one who saved you?" I asked her.

She nodded. "My guardian angel."

At first I thought she was making a joke, but when I looked at her face, I knew she wasn't. She was star-ing at the picture of Sam like it was a picture of Jesus or something. It creeped me out a little.

"Doesn't it make you depressed reading this over and over?" I asked her.

"No," said Sadie, sounding surprised that I would even ask. "It makes me happy." She brought her knees up and wrapped her arms around them. "It makes me feel loved," she said. "He loved me enough to save me."

I followed her eyes to the picture of Sam. Did she really believe he loved her? He didn't even know her when he went in after her. She was just someone who needed saving. She was acting like he was her father, or her boyfriend.

I folded up the article again and handed it to her.

Before she put it back in her pocket, she kissed it, like it was a magic charm or something.

I still can't believe she keeps that thing. It's kind of crazy when you think about it. And I don't understand why she thinks that guy—Sam—loves her. I mean, he was just doing the right thing. I think most people would jump in and try to help someone who was drowning.

Or maybe not. Maybe some people would just stand there and watch. I guess that's why Sadie thinks this guy is so special. But it's still weird that she's all in love with him. I'm not sure who's crazier, her or Rankin. Right now I'd say it's a tie.

DAY 31

If you could change one thing about yourself, what would it be? Just one. It can be anything—a physical thing you wish you had or didn't have, a talent you'd like to have, anything. But you only get one.

That was the question we talked about in group today. You'd think that we all would have picked something to do with why we're here. But mostly we didn't. Juliet said she wished she could play the cello, because she'd like to be able to make people feel the way she does when she hears someone play. Sadie said she wished she could talk to dead people. Rankin said he wished he could throw a perfect spiral pass. And I said I wished I wasn't afraid of heights.

Later, in my one-on-one, Cat Poop asked me if I'd noticed anything different about what I'd said compared to what everyone else said. I thought for a minute but couldn't come up with anything.

"You were the only one who said you wanted to get rid of something," he told me. "Everyone else wanted to add something to themselves, but you wanted to give something up. Why did you say you'd like to get rid of your fear of heights?"

"I don't know," I said. "It was just the first thing that came to me."

It's true, too. I am afraid of heights. I don't even like going up in elevators past about six floors.

"What about that fear makes it the one thing you want to get rid of?" Cat Poop asked me.

I had to think about that for a while. Finally I said, "I guess because it keeps me from doing things I'd like to do."

He asked me what kinds of things, and I told him I've always wanted to try skydiving, or maybe even bungee jumping. "But I'm afraid of heights," I said. "So I can't."

"What is it about heights that you're afraid of?" he asked me.

What a dumb question. Falling, of course. I'm

afraid of falling. That's probably why I dream about it a lot. Actually, what I said to the doc was that I'm afraid that suddenly I'll have this uncontrollable urge to climb up on the railing of the bridge or run to the edge of the cliff or whatever and just throw myself off before anyone can stop me.

Cat Poop wrote something on his pad, which by now we all know means I've said something he thinks is interesting. This time I asked him why he thought my answer was worth writing down. Since it's my life he's dissecting, I figured I had the right to know.

"Why do you think you have this urge to jump?" he said, instead of answering my question.

"I guess because sometimes it's nice to lose control," I said after I'd thought about it. "I feel like I'm always trying to keep control of my life. Sometimes I'd like to be able to just let go and fall."

"Even if it means you might get hurt?" he said.

"I don't think about that," I answered. "I just think about the falling, with no parachute or net or anything to catch me. I just think about falling, and it scares me."

"How about falling in love?" he said. "Are you afraid of that?"

What, is love like the topic of the month around

here or something? It sure didn't take him long to get back to that subject. "I'm only fifteen," I said.

"A lot of people fall in love for the first time around your age," said Cat Poop.

"Why do you want to know?" I said. "Do you have a daughter you want to introduce me to or something?"

He pushed his glasses up his nose. "No," he said. "I don't."

"What if you did?" I asked him. "Would you want her to date a guy like me?"

"That's impossible to answer," Cat Poop said. "I don't have a daughter, so I don't know how I would feel about her dating anyone. It's purely hypothetical."

"Well, purely hypothetically," I said. "Would you want her to date someone like me? Someone who'd been in a place like this?"

Cat Poop scribbled something on his pad. "Are you afraid people won't want to date you because you've been in here?" he asked me.

"I asked you first," I said.

We stared at each other for a while. I guess we were having another game of Psycho Chicken. Anyway, Cat Poop blinked first this time. "I would want my daughter to date the person who made her the happiest," he said.

"Even if that person was crazy?" I said. "Even if that person was like me?"

"If I remember correctly, you've spent a great deal of time telling me you *aren't* crazy," Cat Poop reminded me.

"I'm being hypothetical," I said. "So, would you?"

He sighed. "I don't know," he said.

I laughed. "I didn't think so," I told him.

"Now answer my question," Cat Poop said. "Are you afraid that no one will want to be with you if they know you've spent time here?"

"I don't care what people think," I told him.

"How about what *you* think?" he said.

"I haven't given it a lot of thought," I answered. "Let me get back to you."

"How about Allie?" Cat Poop said. "Do you think she'll still want to be friends with you?"

I didn't know how to answer that one. Allie always said that we'd be best friends no matter what. Was that still true?

"You'd have to ask her," I said.

He let me go after a few more minutes, and he didn't bring up love again, which is really a relief, because I'm getting tired of that subject.

Getting back to the original question, the one about what I would change about myself, it's not really my fear of heights that I'd change. I mean, it's not like that's keeping me from achieving my life's dream of being a tightrope walker or anything. I think it's funny that old Cat Poop got all excited about it, because really it was just something to say.

The truth is, I'd like to have a tail. Seriously. Not a dog tail or a pig tail or anything like that. I want a monkey tail. A long one that I could use to pick stuff up with and hang by. I think that would be completely cool.

Day 32

"What's playing tonight on Nuthouse TV?" I asked Sadie.

As usual, we were in the lounge. Everyone else had gone to bed, even though it wasn't all that late, and except for Moonie, we had the place to ourselves. It reminded me of how sometimes Allie and I stay up late watching movies. Well, how we used to.

Sadie flipped through the channels. "Um, we have a vampire movie, a documentary on whales, or the Home Shopping Network."

"Definitely the Home Shopping Network," I said.

Sadie settled on that channel. The host, a woman with big red hair and an even bigger smile, was showing off some ugly jewelry. She was holding up a ring with a giant fake diamond in it.

"And for only twenty-nine ninety-nine you can have this genuine artificial piece of crap that everyone will know isn't real," I said.

"No fair," said Sadie. "You're supposed to make up something completely different than what it really is."

"That is completely different than what she's really saying," I argued. "She wants us to think that buying that ring will make our lives perfect."

"Maybe it would," Sadie suggested.

"Right," I said, snorting.

"No, really," Sadie said. "Maybe someone out there has been wanting a ring like that their whole life. Now they can get it for twenty-nine ninety-nine."

"Plus shipping and handling," I said. "What's gotten into you?"

"I don't know," Sadie said. "I'm probably just premenstrual or something. It just kind of makes me sad to look at that ring and think that somewhere there's this person who *has* to have it. And I really wish that ring *would* make that person's life better."

"Did you take all your meds today?" I asked her.

Sadie turned the TV off. "Let's just talk," she said.

"About what?" I asked.

"I don't know," said Sadie. "Me. You. Us. Anything."

"I know what this is about," I said. "Cat Poop got into your brain. He's turned you into Therapy Girl."

"Bite me," Sadie said, slapping my leg. "Nobody *talks* around here," she said. "We all pretend to, but we never really do." She pointed to the television. "We're like the people in there," she said, like the TV was an apartment house or something. "We open our mouths, but nothing really comes out."

I'd never heard her talk like this, and to tell the truth, it was a little freaky. I mean, I could always count on Sadie to be sarcastic and funny. Now she was going all Oprah on me.

"Come on," Sadie said. "Tell me a secret."

"Now we're telling secrets?" I said. "What's next, Spin the Bottle?"

"Tell me a secret," she said again, poking her finger into my thigh to punctuate each word.

"Ow!" I said. "Okay. Okay. You win. I'll tell you a secret." Then, before I knew it, I blurted out, "I fooled around with Rankin."

I couldn't believe I'd said it. I didn't mean to. I didn't *want* to. I'd actually been thinking about telling her something about me and Allie. But that's what came out. Afterward, I sat there wishing I could disappear.

"You fooled around with Rankin?" she said.

I almost told her I was kidding. I knew she would believe me if I laughed hard enough to prove it to her. But I didn't. I just nodded. I couldn't say anything. I mean, I'd just told her the worst thing I'd ever done in my entire life.

And do you know what she did? She rolled her eyes.

"You call that a secret?" she said.

"Um, yeah," I said. "Don't you?"

"Well, what do you mean you fooled around?"

"We . . ." I said, then stopped. "We just . . ." I almost told her about sucking Rankin's dick. But I couldn't. So I moved my hand up and down like I was, well, like I was doing what Rankin and I did. The first time.

"You guys jacked off together?" she guessed.

I nodded.

"Wow," she said, and made her eyes really big. For a second I thought she was going to freak out on me, and I started to panic. Then she laughed. "Big news flash," she said. "Guys whack off. Film at eleven."

I didn't know what to say. I thought she would at least be a little surprised. I know she thought me seeing Rankin playing with himself was nothing exciting, but this was different. Totally different. This was *me and Rankin* playing with *each other*. Here I was *totally* freaking out about what happened, and she was treating it like it was nothing. I almost felt like I should apologize for being so boring.

"I meant a secret about *you*," Sadie said.

"That *was* about me!" I said.

"No," said Sadie. "It was just something you did that you think people would be freaked out about if they knew. Trust me, everybody around here has done stuff way weirder than that."

"Like what?" I asked.

"Remember Alice?" said Sadie.

Like I could ever forget. I nodded.

"She used to catch flies—and *eat* them. And last time I was here there was this guy named Benny. He liked to hide things up his butt. Trust me, what you and Rankin did was so *not* secret-worthy."

I looked at her while she waited for me to respond. "Sorry," I said. "It's all I've got." Which wasn't true, but for some reason I wanted to stop while I actually felt a little better. I was afraid if I told Sadie the rest, suddenly it wouldn't be so "normal."

"How about what happened between you and Allie?" she said.

"What do you mean?"

"Come on," Sadie said. "I know you did what you did because something happened between the two of you. So what was it? You can tell me. Since we're sharing and everything."

"There's nothing to tell," I said. To tell the truth, in a weird way I was kind of pissed off that she didn't think the thing with Rankin was a real secret. I mean, even if it *wasn't* a big deal, and even if I did feel a little better about it now, it was still a secret.

Sadie clearly wasn't buying my cool act. "Yeah, there is," she argued. "What? You slept with her and she freaked out? You and that Burke guy got into a fight over her? What was it?"

"I told you, it had nothing to do with her," I said.

I thought she would push me some more, but she didn't. She just looked at me for a long time. I looked right back at her. I've gotten pretty good at staring contests what with the doc and I having one practically every day. The trick is to sort of unfocus your eyes so that you're looking at the person but not really *seeing* them. If you do it right, they can never tell.

That's how I won the staring contest with Sadie. After a minute she just turned away and turned the TV back on. The sound was still off, so we sat and watched the host talk. Now she was pitching some fake pearl necklace.

Sadie was quiet for so long that I thought maybe she was pissed at me. I was just about to say something when she started talking again.

"Remember that Saturday morning cartoon show with all the superheroes?" she asked. "Wonder Woman, Aquaman, Superman?"

"Sure," I said. "*Super Friends.* What about it?"

Sadie stared at the television. "They all looked like normal people until they turned into these other things, right? But it always turned out that they originally turned into superheroes when they were running from something they didn't like about themselves. Like Batman fought the dark part of his soul by battling bad guys and all that."

"I think Wonder Woman was just born Wonder Woman," I argued. "And Superman was just Superman."

"Okay," Sadie said. "Bad examples. But think about the really interesting superheroes. Most of them were normal until they turned into something freaky. Like Wolverine. He was part of some experiment. And the guy who turned into the Hulk hated to do it because it meant he was mad. Plus, it hurt."

"I guess so," I admitted.

Sadie went on. "When I was a kid, I used to watch that show, sitting on the couch in my pajamas and wishing more than anything that one day I'd just change into this other person," she said. "I thought that would explain everything. You know, about why I felt so different. Then I'd find out that my mother was really an alien or that I'd been bitten by a radioactive spider as a baby, and it would all be okay because I'd be able to fly and see through walls."

She stopped talking and watched the TV some more. I thought that I should say something, but then she started talking again. "But it never happened," she said. "I just went on being me my whole life, until one day I realized that all those superheroes were doing was fighting themselves, and that getting to breathe underwater or shoot fire from your fingers didn't really make up for being screwed up in the first place. It was just the consolation prize—you got the great costume and the invisible jet for being a loser in everything else."

She stared at the silent TV. Her expression was completely blank, as if her soul had just flown out of her body. It was actually kind of scary. "I guess I just want my invisible jet," she said.

Day 33

Now I know for sure that all of this is a dream, because what happened tonight can't possibly be real. It just can't.

I don't even know where to start. Rankin came into my room last night. I guess technically it was earlier today, since it must have been about one or two in the morning. I was sleeping, and then I felt something pressing against my back. Rankin had pulled my shorts down, and he was pushing himself against me. I was still only half awake, so I didn't realize what he was doing at first. He put his arms around me and pulled me closer. I could hear him breathing in my ear.

Believe it or not, that's not even the bad thing. If

that was all, I could probably handle it. Probably. But that was just the beginning.

Like I said, Rankin was holding on to me and trying to . . . I don't think I can even say it right now. But he was getting close. As soon as I realized what he was doing, I woke up fast. I even opened my mouth to tell him to stop.

And that's when the screaming started.

At first I thought it was me screaming. Then I realized it was a girl's voice. I don't know what Rankin thought was going on, but he pulled me closer to him and put his hand on my mouth. Maybe he thought I was the one screaming too.

It was so weird. I was trying to figure out who was screaming and I was trying to get Rankin off me all at the same time. Everything was happening at once, but I felt like I couldn't even move because I didn't know what was more important, getting away from Rankin or helping whoever was making the awful noise.

That's when the light came on. It snapped on like fireworks exploding over our heads. I couldn't see. Rankin rolled off of me and sat on the edge of the bed, covering himself with his hands. I looked up and saw Carl and Nurse Moon standing in the doorway. The screaming had stopped, like the light switch controlled that too.

"Pull your shorts up, Jeff," Moonie said. She wasn't yelling or anything. She said it really calmly.

I pulled up my underwear. Rankin had picked his up from the floor and was pulling them on. I glanced over at Nurse Moon and saw that she was looking down to give him some privacy. Carl, though, was staring at us. Staring at us and shaking his head, like we were his grandkids and we'd just disappointed him big time.

"Rankin, back to your room," Nurse Moon said when he was dressed.

Rankin didn't look at me as he walked out of the room. He didn't look at Moonie or Carl either. He rushed by them and down the hall. I looked at Nurse Moon, my heart pounding in my chest.

"What's going on?" I asked. "Who was screaming?"

"It's Martha," Moonie told me.

That scared me. "Is she all right?" I asked. "What happened? Is she hurt?" I started to go toward the door.

"Don't you worry about her," said Nurse Moon, holding up her hand so that I stopped. "She had a bad dream. That's all."

I nodded. I know all about dreams that make you want to scream. Then I remembered why Carl and Nurse Moon were in my room in the first place.

"We were just . . ." I began.

Moonie interrupted me. "Dr. Katzrupus will talk to you in the morning," she said. "Good night."

That was it. Good night. Like she was tucking me in. No yelling. No "*I'm very disappointed in you.*" No nothing. And you know what? That was worse. If she'd yelled, or seemed disgusted, or even at all upset, I would have felt better. But she treated it like she didn't care. Like it didn't matter.

Maybe it doesn't. I don't know anymore. Maybe Sadie is right and it's just something guys do. Maybe it doesn't *mean* anything. I'd really rather not talk about it with Cat Poop, though. It's exactly the kind of thing he writes about on his stupid pad.

When I finally fell asleep after Moonie left, I had the weirdest dream.

First we were in group—all of us, even the people who are gone now. Cat Poop asked us to go around the circle and say what we were most afraid of. Alice said she was afraid of being alone. Bone said he was afraid of cars, which seemed weird until I remembered the whole gas station thing. Juliet said she was afraid of teeth, which because she's Juliet didn't seem strange at all. Rankin said he was afraid of losing. Martha didn't say anything.

Sadie said she wasn't afraid of anything, and I believed her. In my dream it was like she had this force field around her that protected her from everything the rest of us have to watch out for. Then she looked at me and said, "Once you realize there's nothing to be afraid of when you die, there's nothing else to worry about."

When it was my turn, I couldn't think of anything to say. I looked around at the rest of the group and thought how messed up they all were. Then I looked at my wrists and realized that they were bleeding again. I pulled my sleeves down to cover them, but I could feel the blood soaking through, and I was afraid everyone was going to notice and start laughing at me.

When I woke up from the dream, I felt weird. I can't really explain it. There was this knot in my stomach, the same kind I get when I wake up the morning of a big test I know I haven't studied enough for. Then I remembered Rankin, and that I was going to have to talk to Cat Poop about what happened, and I knew why the knot was there.

Day 34

I'll never know what Sadie would have thought about my dream. I was going to tell her, but she . . .

No. Wait. I have to start at the beginning. If I don't, I'm going to get everything mixed up, because right now it's all swirling around in my brain. I can catch bits and pieces of it, but trying to see the whole picture at once is really hard. I don't even know if I want to see it. If I see it, I might fall apart.

So yesterday morning, after the famous Jeff and Rankin Get Busted incident, I got dressed and walked down the hall to the lounge. (I did *not* take a shower, which is a little gross, but I don't exactly have a great track record in that department lately.) Part of me expected everyone to be lined up, waiting to tell me how awful I was before they threw me out. But no one else was up. Instead, Goody was sitting at the desk, reading a file. I wondered if it was mine, and if she knew what had happened.

"Dr. Katzrupus is waiting for you in his office," she said, answering that question.

I walked down the hall to Cat Poop's door and knocked. He opened it and I walked into his office, not saying anything or even looking at him. I sat down in the chair across from his desk and waited for him to tell me I was leaving.

"Do you want to talk about what happened last night?" he said.

"Not really," I told him. "But I'll bet a million bucks that you do."

He nodded. "Do you have anything to say about it?"

I shook my head.

"Let me ask you this," said Cat Poop. "How did it happen?"

"What do you mean, how did it happen?"

"How did it happen?" he repeated. "I think it's a pretty straightforward question."

I kind of huffed at him. It was a stupid question, is what it was. I shrugged. "He came into my room, got

223

into my bed, and tried to butt burgle me," I said.

Cat Poop pushed his glasses up. "You're sure?" he asked.

"Of course I'm sure," I answered. "Trust me, if some guy tries to stick his junk in you, you know it."

"I meant that you're certain you didn't encourage Rankin in any way."

I had to think about that one. I mean, Rankin's the one who's started it every time we've done anything. But it's not like he's ever *forced* me to do it, and until last night I've never exactly told him *not* to do what he's done. Maybe if I had, he wouldn't have kept trying. But I didn't want to tell Cat Poop that. It would just make me look like a victim, and he'd want to talk about it even more.

"Are you suggesting that I asked for it because I wore my sexy boxers?" I asked instead.

"I spoke to Rankin this morning," said the doc. "He said that it was you who talked him into doing it."

"What?" I said. "He said *I* started it?"

I couldn't believe that Rankin had lied. Well, yes, I could. Still, I was pissed off. "It was *not* my idea," I said, more to myself than to Cat Poop. "He's the one who came to *my* room. He's the one who's a—"

I stopped myself from saying it. But I thought it. A

224

fag. Rankin was the fag around here. Not me.

Cat Poop pushed his glasses up his nose again. I almost told him to knock it off. "Jeff, I have to tell you that this is a serious breach of hospital rules. You could be asked to leave the program."

"Finally," I muttered. "If I'd known that, I would have done it a long time ago."

"Unless," said the doc, "there's some other reason for your behavior. Something that relates to your overall reason for being here."

It took me a minute to understand what he was saying. When I did, I got mad. "Nice," I said. "You're trying to get me to talk by threatening to kick me out for something I didn't do. Where'd they teach you that, shrink torture school?"

Cat Poop leaned forward. "All I'm asking you is if what you did with Rankin has any connection to why you hurt yourself," he said.

"No," I said instantly. "It has nothing to do with it. I mean, I fooled around with Sadie, too, and that didn't mean . . ."

I stopped, realizing that I'd just made a huge mistake.

"You and Sadie—" Cat Poop started to say. His finger was already halfway to his nose.

"No," I interrupted. "I didn't mean it like that."

"What exactly *did* you mean?" he asked.

I searched around in my head for some answer to give him, anything that could erase what I'd already said. But I knew I couldn't. I'd gone too far.

"All right," I said. "Yeah, I fooled around with Sadie. But I couldn't." I looked at my hands, which were in my lap. My fingers were wrestling with each other.

"Couldn't what?"

I forced my hands to be still. "Couldn't, you know, *do* it," I mumbled. "And with Rankin it was just fooling around. Nothing serious. It's not like I'm in love with him or anything. Not like it was with . . ."

Again I realized too late that I'd slipped up. That made twice in less than five minutes. If I didn't do damage control, and fast, I was basically going to make sure I was on the next bus out of there. And for some reason, I didn't want to be on that bus.

"With whom?" Cat Poop asked.

"Nobody," I said. "I was just talking."

"With Allie?" he said.

I could feel his eyes on me. I started to say that, yeah, it was Allie. But I didn't. I didn't say anything. He was starting to win, and I didn't want him to win. I wanted to be the winner, even if it meant letting him think I'd come on to Rankin or whatever.

And that's when he dropped the bomb. "Jeff," he said. "I have to tell you something. About Sadie."

"I know we shouldn't have—" I said, trying to head him off. It was bad enough that I was probably going to get kicked out. I didn't want to be responsible for Sadie having to leave, too. So I just kept talking, hoping it would make him change his mind. "That time it *was* my idea. I'm the one who went into her room. She didn't come into mine. And really, it was no big thing, anyway. I was just feeling lonely. You can even ask her."

"Jeff, listen," he said. His voice sounded weird, and suddenly I wanted to be anywhere but in his office. The way he looked reminded me of the way my dad looked the time he had to tell Amanda that her cat got hit by a car.

"What?" I asked. "Did she leave already? Did you kick her out? Because I'm telling the truth. You can't just—"

"Jeff," Cat Poop interrupted. "Sadie's dead."

I knew he hadn't just said that. I mean, there was no way he could have said it. "*Sadie's dead*?" No. I was sure I'd heard wrong. He'd said "*Sadie's gone*." That's what he'd said.

227

"What do you mean?" I asked him. "You mean she *left*."

"Last night," he said. "You heard the screaming, right?"

"But that was Martha," I said. "Moon Face said it was Martha."

He nodded. "It *was* Martha," he said.

"She had a bad dream," I said.

Cat Poop actually took off his glasses. It was the first time he's ever done that, and it made him look naked. Naked and tired. Then I realized that he hadn't shaved. It was like he'd been up all night. He rubbed his eyes for a minute before talking again.

"Martha went to Sadie's room," he said. "I imagine she *did* have a bad dream and wanted to be comforted. She found Sadie."

"Found her what?" I asked him, not understanding.

He shook his head. "Dead," he said. Flat. Just like that. "She found Sadie dead."

I laughed. I know it sounds weird, but I did. "You're kidding," I said. "You'd better be kidding. Because Sadie is *not* dead. She's waiting to have breakfast with me. It's pancake day."

"I'm sorry," said Cat Poop. "I know this is very difficult for you to hear and accept, particularly under the circumstances. And I wouldn't have told you now, but—"

"Under the circumstances?" I said. Then I started laughing again. I don't know why. It just started pouring out of me, this loud laughter. Like some kind of crazy clown. I don't think I was even thinking anything. I was just laughing.

And then it turned into crying. I was crying. Just bawling my eyes out. Then the next thing I know, Cat Poop was beside me. He actually hugged me. And I let him. I let him hug me while I bawled. I still didn't believe him about Sadie. But I cried anyway. After a while I didn't even know why I was crying. I didn't know if it was because of the Rankin thing or the Sadie thing or the Jeff thing. And it didn't matter. It just felt good.

I don't know how long I cried, but it felt like a hundred hours. I think part of me thought that if I just kept crying none of it would be real. Sadie wouldn't be dead. The stuff with Rankin would never have happened. I wouldn't be crazy.

But she is. And it did. And I am.

Day 35

So about the whole trying-to-kill-myself thing. I guess there's no reason not to talk about it now. It's not like things can get any worse.

I did it on New Year's Eve. I had the best idea, too. I wanted to get drunk along with all the people in Times Square, then do it as the ball fell. You know, slip away with the old year into wherever it goes when it's used up and we throw it away. So maybe it's a little dramatic, but hey, you've got to appreciate the thought.

And, no, I didn't actually do it in Times Square. That would just be too weird. I did it at home. In my bedroom. Watching it all on TV.

The whiskey was a good start. I got the idea from

Dylan Thomas. He's this poet who drank twenty-one straight whiskeys at The White Horse Tavern in New York and then died on the spot from alcohol poisoning. I've always wanted to hear the bartender's side of the story. What was it like watching this guy drink himself out of here? How did it feel handing him number twenty-one and watching his face crumple up before he fell off the stool? And did he already have number twenty-two poured, waiting for that big fat tip, and then have to drink it himself after whoever came took the body away?

So I drank some whiskey. I don't see how Dylan Thomas choked down twenty-one glasses of the stuff. I could barely drink three. But that was enough. It made everything seem okay somehow, like killing myself was the best idea I'd ever had. I wasn't afraid.

Cutting myself felt so good. It was sweet the way the razor opened up the skin and this red line appeared, like I was pulling a piece of thread out of my wrist. The blood came really slowly, not in some spastic blast like I thought it would. It didn't even really feel like my arm. It was like I was watching someone else's arm in a movie. I kept thinking how great the camera angle was and wishing I had some popcorn.

The people on television were counting down the

seconds until the new year. What a bunch of morons they all were, acting excited to have another whole year, but having to get trashed so they wouldn't think about how they were going to screw it up again like they had all the other years. Everyone was looking up at the top of the building as though Jesus Christ himself had appeared and was tossing out chocolate-covered salvation, like just because some crazy glitter ball was falling on their heads it gave them another chance to be happy. Only I could tell them it never changed, that no matter how many glitter balls fell in New York City, the year would still suck and their lives would still be screwed up and everything would still turn out wrong.

"Use the razor!" I shouted at the television. "Use the razor!" But none of them did. Just me.

That's when I did the other wrist, and that was even better because I knew—knew what it would feel like, knew what would happen. Man, did it feel good, like slicing open the ribbon on a Christmas present you've been staring at under the tree for a month and been dying to open. Then it's finally time to open it, and you just kind of hold your breath while you rip off the paper, hoping that what's inside will be what you want it to be. And for once, it was.

Afterward I just lay there watching everyone kiss

while I died, thinking how cool it was to be on my bedroom floor bleeding while everyone in America celebrated the end of my life and the idiot hosting the countdown smiled his goofy fake smile on the TV like the Angel of Death doing a toothpaste commercial. There was none of that tunnel-of-light crap either. No angels waiting to lead me over. It was just dark and quiet.

That's when I woke up and saw my parents bending over me. At first I thought I was dreaming. My mother still had on all her makeup and her party dress, and there were these great big streaks of purple eye shadow down her cheeks and her lipstick was all smeared and she looked like a freaked-out Grow 'N Style Barbie head my sister had when she was about eight. You know, that life-size plastic head of Barbie where you can put makeup on it and fix its hair with curlers. Amanda and I used to play with it a lot until the day our next-door neighbor, an older kid named Troy, found us doing it and called me a fag. Later on I buried it in the backyard.

So my mother's looking down at me saying, "Why, why, why," over and over again, like some little kid keeps pulling the string that makes her talk. My father isn't saying anything at all; he's just looking at me like

233

maybe *he's* the one who's dreaming. That's when I realized that I wasn't dead, that I was still on the floor in my room. And all I could do was look at my mother's mouth opening and closing and wonder if I could make her say something else, like one of those See 'n Say toys where you point the arrow to the picture of the chick and it says, "The chick goes 'cluck, cluck, cluck.'" And I started to laugh, thinking about it, about her clucking nonstop, and she cried these big purple tears that splashed against my face like rain.

The next time I opened my eyes I was in this room. The same one I'm in now, staring at the same ceiling I'm staring at right now. Looking at the Devil's face. It was snowing outside my window and Nurse Goody was sitting in the chair next to my bed, looking at me like I was an exhibit at the Museum of Natural History and she was searching for the little brass plaque that would tell her what I was and when I became extinct.

So that's it. That's the big secret. I tried to kill myself on New Year's Eve. Just like Sadie did last night. Only she really did it. I don't know all the details, just the basics. She took a bunch of pills. I don't know what they were or where she got them. I'd like to think they were Wonder Drug. Then at least she could have gone thinking she was flying.

234

Day 36

My mother started right off with the hugging, like now that she's started doing it, she can't stop.

"We were so sorry to hear that your friend is gone," she said, patting me on the back.

At first I thought she meant Rankin, who got sent home because of what happened. I guess Cat Poop decided I was the one telling the truth, because I'm still here. Or maybe they flipped a coin and I won. Or lost. Anyway, he's gone. I don't miss him.

When I thought my mother was talking about him, I felt my heart stop for a second. I really didn't want to talk about him. Us. Whatever. Anyway, then I realized that she meant Sadie, and my heart started beating again. But then I went from being scared to being angry. I wanted to say, "She's not just *gone*, she's DEAD!" But I knew she was trying to make me feel better, so I just didn't say anything.

I wasn't exactly looking forward to the weekly Family Frolic, what with everything that's been going on. Thankfully, my parents brought Amanda with them. I was really glad to see her. She was kind of a guarantee that I wouldn't just lose it. But even she was a little less Amandaish than usual. I think she thought she should be because of Sadie and everything.

Cat Poop started out by reminding us all that I only have nine more days here. As if I didn't know that. Five weeks ago nine days in this place might as well have been a thousand years to me. Now it seems like nothing.

"The house has really changed since you've been in the . . . since you've been gone," my father said. "I can't wait for you to see it." He had his hands in his lap, and he kept twirling his thumbs, which is what he does when he doesn't want to be doing whatever it is he's doing. I'm sure he wanted out of there as much as I did, and I kind of felt sorry for him. I guess it must be hard knowing your kid tried to kill himself.

"Right," said my mother. She was being super

chirpy, the way she is when she wants to pretend everything's fine. "We put new carpeting in your bedroom. It's a beautiful color. What color would you say it is, Amanda?"

Amanda looked at her. "Beige," she said. "It's beige."

"Oh, I think it's more sand," my mother said. "Isn't that what the salesman said it was called: desert sand? Anyway, it looks wonderful with the paint. Amanda, what would you call that shade of blue?"

"Blue," said Amanda, looking at me and rolling her eyes. "I'd call it blue."

I knew this was my mother's way of letting me know I won't have to look at any bloodstains when I go back. It doesn't really matter if the stains are there or not, though. I'm still going to remember. But it's nice of her to think of it.

Then Cat Poop said he'd discussed with my parents the idea of me going to a different school, so that I could have a fresh start. He wanted to know how I felt about that.

I said it was a lot to think about, and that I'd get back to them on it. I kind of like the idea of going somewhere new. It would give me a chance to start over, to be anybody I want to be. But that's the thing: I don't

237

want to be anybody. I want to be me. I don't know if that would be any easier at a new school or not.

I mean, yeah, I'm a little scared about the stories I'm sure are going around. Probably by now someone has a website up about me. www.jefftriedtokillhimself.com. With pictures. And a blog. And part of me would be totally relieved not to have to walk into my old school and see everyone looking at my wrists. Seriously, how long can you get away with never wearing T-shirts?

But would it really be any better in a new place? Maybe at first. But sooner or later someone would find out what happened to me. That's just how it is. Some kid will know someone who knows someone from my old school, and pretty soon the stories will start flying around. Then I'll walk into school one day and hear all of this whispering as I walk through the halls.

That's what happened when Ginny Mangerman went away for a few months. Her sister told everyone Ginny was doing a semester as an exchange student in Australia, but it turned out she was pregnant and went somewhere to have the baby and give it up for adoption. By the time she came back, everyone knew what had happened. Someone thought it would be funny to cut out pictures of babies from magazines and paste them all over her locker. Ginny ended up dropping out, and now she works at a supermarket as a checkout girl. I try to be really nice to her when I get in her line, but she pretends she doesn't recognize anyone from school.

It's probably better to just go back to my old school and deal with it. Amanda still goes there, and I don't want her to be the one who gets teased because I can't face anyone. I know she could handle it, but she shouldn't have to. Maybe we can both go somewhere new. Or maybe I can convince my parents to move to France. No one in France cares if you tried to kill yourself. In fact, I think they like you better because you're all tragic.

This is all the stuff I was thinking while my mother was talking about how great it will be to have me back. Then I guess even Cat Poop got tired of hearing her talk, because all of a sudden he asked Amanda, "How do you feel about your brother coming home?"

I was actually curious to hear what she had to say, and not just because it meant my mother would have to shut up for a minute.

"I can't wait," Amanda said. "I'm tired of having to do the dishes by myself."

I laughed inside. I knew she said that to be a smart-ass. She can be worse than I am when she tries.

But she was totally giving everyone this serious face, so they didn't know whether to believe her or not.

"Do you have anything you'd like to ask Jeff?" Cat Poop asked her, trying again. Since he's dealt with me for so long now, he probably knows Amanda operates the same way I do. I waited for him to start doing the staring thing with her.

But Amanda didn't look at him; she looked at me. I could tell she was trying not to laugh, so I did my best to look really serious, too. She waited a minute, just kind of biting her lip, like she was thinking about something deep. Then she said, "If you do it again, can I have your room?"

"Amanda!" my mother said, shocked. My father stopped twirling his thumbs and looked like he wanted to die. Cat Poop got his pencil ready.

"What?" Amanda said, acting all innocent.

"I don't think Jeff appreciated that," said my father.

But I did. See, this was kind of an in-joke with us. When we first moved into our house, Amanda and I both wanted the bigger bedroom. She said she should have it because she's a girl and it has its own bathroom. I said I should have it because I'm older. I ended up locking myself in the room, and stayed there practically a whole day until my parents said I could have it. I was all ready to rub it in, but then I found out that Amanda had set me up. She knew I would fight her for the room, and she only pretended to be upset about not getting it because what she really wanted was a new bike and horseback riding lessons, both of which my parents gave her when she boo-hooed about her whole life being totally unfair. She's good.

I played along. "It's okay," I said in this calm voice. They all looked at me. I think they expected me to give some big speech about how I have no intention of ever trying it again. Instead I said, like it was really hard for me to get the words out, "You can totally have my room if I ever kill myself again."

"Jeff!" my mother and father said at the same time. Then my mother looked at Cat Poop. "You see what we live with?" she said. "The two of them . . ."

"I think Amanda and Jeff understand each other quite well," said the doc before she could finish. When I looked at him, he pushed his glasses up. I thought he might be smiling a little, but he wiped his mouth with his hand, and when he brought it away, he looked like his old shrinky self.

"Well, I wish *we* understood them," my mother said.

Amanda looked at me again, and that's when I

realized that what she thought of me was more important than what anybody else thought. Isn't that weird? And I can't tell you why it is. Maybe because I don't want her to be afraid of me. I think I could handle it if the kids at school were afraid of me. Even my parents. But Amanda's different. I want her to know she can trust me. One day she might really need me for something, and I don't want her to be afraid to ask.

The rest of the session was boring. Cat Poop talked a lot about "transitioning from the therapeutic environment to the home environment" and crap like that. Mostly I made faces at Amanda when no one was looking and tried to get her to crack up. She did, once, but then she started coughing to cover it up.

When it was all over, there was more hugging. When it came time for me and Amanda to hug, I held her really tight and whispered in her ear, "Next time I'm going to do it on *your* carpet."

She had to pretend to cough again so my parents wouldn't hear us laughing. But I think she knew I was really telling her that she didn't have to worry. As they all left, I heard my mother say to her, "I think we should take you to Dr. Leach tomorrow. It sounds like you're coming down with something." Amanda turned and glared at me, and I just waved at her.

"Would you mind staying a little longer today?" Cat Poop asked as I was getting ready to go back to my room. "I thought we might talk some more."

I knew that he knew that there was more to my story than what I'd already told him. And suddenly I was really, really tired. Not of talking to him, but of *not* talking to him. I was tired of all the games I'd been playing, and of holding back. Maybe realizing how much I wanted Amanda to believe that I was okay is what did it. Maybe it was Sadie being dead, or Rankin being gone. I don't really know. But I knew I was ready to talk.

I sat down. "Okay," I said. "Where should I start?"

"Where every good story starts," said Cat Poop. "At the beginning."

DAY 37

No one ever tells you that when your heart breaks, you can feel it. But you can. It feels like something has crumbled inside you and the pieces are falling into your stomach. It hurts more than any punch ever could. You stop breathing, and for a while you can't remember how. When you finally do, it feels like your throat has closed up, like you're trying to suck air through a straw.

I tried to kill myself because of what happened with Burke. Not Allie and Burke. *Me* and Burke. During Christmas break.

It really started a couple of months before that. I guess you could say I had a crush on Burke. Actually, it's not even a guess—I *did* have a crush on Burke. Big-time.

When Burke first asked Allie out, I was happy for her. I knew she liked him, and she was so excited when he finally talked to her. Besides, it was just a movie. She even asked me to go along. She said it was so she wouldn't be tempted to do too much with Burke. She'd read in some magazine that guys will be more interested if you play it cool, and that the best way to do that is to go on group dates where you can't exactly climb all over each other without someone giving you a hard time about it. I was her group.

The funny thing is, Burke didn't mind. The three of us went to a movie. I don't even remember what it was. Burke sat in the middle. There I was, right next to him, with Allie on his other side. He even shared his popcorn with me. It was like the three of us were on a date, although I didn't think about that then. I just thought it was cool of him.

I remember reaching into the popcorn about halfway through the movie. Burke reached in at the same time, and for a few seconds our fingers touched. I don't remember who pulled away first, but I remember feeling this strange sensation. I don't even know what to call it. A tickle maybe, in my stomach. I put my fingers in my mouth and sucked the fake butter off, like I was trying to find out what Burke tasted like. I didn't touch that popcorn for the rest of the movie.

After that, Allie started spending more time with Burke. At first they almost always asked me along. Then one night Allie went out alone with him. She didn't even tell me she was going, but she called me when she got home. "He kissed me," she said. She sounded all excited, like she'd just won a million dollars.

"He did?" I asked her. "Why?"

"What do you mean *why*?" said Allie. She laughed, like it was the dumbest question anyone could ask. "Because he wanted to."

She told me all about it. They went for a walk. Burke bought them ice cream cones. He joked around, getting ice cream on her nose. Then he licked it off. And then he kissed her. I remember exactly what she said. "His lips were soft, like a kitten." I thought that was a really weird way to describe someone's lips. At the same time, I knew exactly what she meant.

I tried to be excited for her. But the whole time I was telling her how happy I was for her, I was really thinking that I wanted it to be my nose Burke was licking ice cream off and me kissing his kitten lips. And the more I thought about that, the more scared I got. I think that was the first time I realized that I didn't just like Burke, I had a thing for him.

After that, I didn't want to be around Burke and Allie. At least not when they were together. It was too much. Every time I saw Burke I couldn't stop thinking about how much I liked him. He's got these amazing brown eyes and a killer smile. When he looks at you, you feel like he's really *looking* at you, if you know what I mean. I wanted him to look at me like that all the time.

But of course he was always looking at Allie. And she was always talking about him. To me. And there was absolutely no way I could tell her why I didn't want to hear it. So for a few months I was all crushed out on him and totally miserable. I got jealous every time Allie talked about him or when I saw them holding hands or kissing.

Then, right before Christmas, the three of us were at this party at Rebecca Miller's house. Her parents were out of town, which means we were drinking a little. Or in my case, a lot. I think I had a couple of beers, which really does a number on your head when you're not used to drinking.

The weird thing is that I felt happy and sad all at

the same time. The more beer I drank and the more I watched Allie with Burke, the more confused I got. I wanted my best friend back. But I also couldn't stop wondering what it would be like for Burke to be as into me as he was into Allie. I'd never thought about another guy like that—or about *anybody* like that. The truth is, I didn't think about sex all that much, because when I did, it scared me. It wasn't until that night at the party that I knew *why* it scared me.

When I realized what I was feeling, I thought I might be sick, so I went upstairs to the bathroom where no one would hear me. I knelt in front of the toilet and waited for everything to come up. I remember my head was spinning a little. I closed my eyes, but that just made it worse, so I hung over the bowl, staring at the water and feeling my insides churn.

I didn't throw up, though, and after a while I felt a little bit better. I stood up and looked at myself in the mirror. I hated what I saw. I wanted to punch the guy in the mirror in the face for being such a freak. It was like I wasn't even looking at myself, I was looking at someone I'd never seen before, someone I didn't want to see ever again.

That's when the door opened. I'd forgotten to lock it. And before I could say something, in walked Burke.

He looked at me and smiled this big, almost-drunk smile. "Hey, man," he said. "You done?"

I couldn't say anything, so I just nodded.

"Cool," he said. "I need to take a major leak."

He didn't wait for me to leave. He walked over to the toilet, unzipped, and pulled himself out. I tried not to look, but I couldn't help it. I didn't even care if he saw me looking, but he didn't notice anything. When he was done, he turned around and looked at me while he zipped up.

"You look wasted, buddy," he said, grinning again.

He was standing right in front of me. Even drunk, he was beautiful. "This party is killer, isn't it?" he said. His breath smelled like beer, but I didn't care.

"Yeah," I said. "Killer." I wanted to get out of that bathroom, but I couldn't leave. My feet wouldn't move.

"Hey," said Burke. "There's something I want to ask you."

My heart did this weird flip-flop thing when he said that. For a second—just a split second—I had this idea that he was going to ask me out. I don't know why, but I imagined him asking me to go to a movie or something. And the thing is, at that moment I really wanted him to. I remembered the popcorn, and his fingers, and that tingling feeling hit me again.

"What?" I said, barely able to get the word out.

Burke looked all serious for a second. "It's about Allie," he said. He sounded nervous, which wasn't like him at all. Burke doesn't get nervous. He's always cool. Then *I* got even more nervous, because I was imagining all kinds of things he could say next.

Burke looked right into my eyes. Everything stopped while I waited for him to ask me his question. Then he said, "What should I get her for Christmas?"

It took me a few seconds to understand what he'd said. When it finally registered, I was surprised at how sad I was. But I couldn't let him know that. I had to think of something to say. "Uh, she likes clothes," I said.

Burke shook his head. "I'm no good at picking out that shit," he told me.

"I can go with you," I said before I knew it. "We can pick something out together." As soon as I said it, I felt like a moron. What kind of guy tells another guy he'll go shopping with him? But all I could think about right then was how much I wanted to do something with Burke. Anything. Even shop for his girlfriend's Christmas present. That's how I was thinking of Allie, as his girlfriend. Not *my* best friend.

Burke laughed. "Cool," he said, like it was the most normal thing in the world. "Cool." Then he patted my arm. "You're a cool guy," he said.

My heart was racing so fast I thought I might be having a heart attack.

And then I did it. I couldn't stop myself. Burke was touching my arm, we'd just made a kind of date, and I was suddenly happier than I'd ever been in my whole life. Before I even knew what I was doing, I leaned forward and kissed him right on the mouth. I remember thinking, for the few seconds our lips were touching, that Allie had been right. His lips were as soft as a kitten.

He pushed me away, but not hard. "Hey there," he said, kind of laughing. "Don't get all gay on me. It's not like I asked you out or something." He laughed again.

I didn't say anything. I've never been so scared in my life. Not because of what I thought he might do, but because of what *I'd* done. I tried to think of something to say to him to make it all go away, something to explain why I'd kissed him, but I knew there was nothing that would erase that kiss.

I guess Burke saw that I wasn't laughing with him. He stopped laughing and his eyebrows wrinkled up, like he just realized he'd been tricked. "What's up?"

he asked. He stared into my eyes for a few seconds. "Wait," he said then, pulling back and looking at me as if he'd never seen me before. "Are you a fag?"

Now, I'd been called a fag before. But not in the way Burke meant it. Sometimes guys just say that, like "You're such a fag," meaning you're doing something lame. Burke meant something else, though. Suddenly, that word was the most dangerous word in the English language.

I tried to answer him. "I . . . I really like you," I said.

Burke stepped back. "Holy shit," he said. He had this look on his face that terrified me. "Holy shit," he said again.

"Burke," I said, reaching out to him. "Burke, don't . . ."

He put his hands up, blocking me from getting any nearer. He shook his head. "You *are* a fag," he said.

He pushed past me and left the bathroom. A few seconds later, everything in my stomach came up. I puked all over the floor and all over myself. It felt like I was throwing up my heart. I was crying and couldn't breathe, and I wanted to be dead.

I cleaned up the mess on the floor with some towels, but my clothes were still all dirty. I just wanted to get out of there. That's when I remembered that to get out I would have to go down the stairs and through the party. Allie would be there, and I knew that by now Burke would have told her what happened. What I was. I couldn't face her.

I thought about going out the window, but I was still feeling like crap, and I was afraid I'd fall and make things even worse. Finally I went into the hall. I stood at the top of the stairs, listening to the people laughing below me. I imagined they were laughing at me, that Burke had told them all about how I'd kissed him, about how I was a fag, and that they thought it was the funniest thing they'd ever heard. I just knew they were all waiting for the big fag to appear so that they could make fun of me.

There was nothing else to do. I went down those stairs as quickly as I could and went straight for the door. I didn't look at anyone, and prayed no one would stop me. And they didn't. That's the only good thing that happened that night. No one stopped me. I made it to the door and out of that house, and then I ran home and up to my room.

I haven't seen Allie since then. I've talked to her, though. When I didn't hear from her for three days, I knew that Burke had told her. On Christmas Eve, when I couldn't take it any more, I called her. When she answered I said, "I just want to say Merry Christmas."

She didn't say anything for a while. I could hear her breathing. Then she said, "Why didn't you tell me you're gay?"

"I'm not," I said. "Allie, you have to believe me."

"I thought we were friends," she said, and hung up. That's the last thing she ever said to me.

So now you know the whole story about why I got all dramatic on New Year's Eve, and why I'm here. I'm gay. I know it sounds stupid. Tons of people are gay, and you'd think it would be no big deal. But I was really hoping I wasn't, that it was all just a big mix-up and I'd get over it. After the stuff with Rankin, and what happened—or didn't happen—with Sadie, though, I know that I won't get over it. It's what I am.

I read once that a third of all gay kids try to kill themselves. They say it's because being gay is so hard in this world. They say that we won't stop trying to kill ourselves until more people understand us, and until we live in a world where it's okay for a guy to love another guy. That's probably true. But there will never be a world where it's okay to fall in love with your best friend's boyfriend.

Day 38

So now we've established that not only did I try to kill myself, but that I'm gay, too. That's like having two cherries on your dog crap sundae. Or extra nuts.

And now, of course, it's all Cat Poop wants to talk about. Today he asked me to tell him more about what Rankin and I did together. It was completely embarrassing talking about that. Then he asked me how I felt about having sex. I told him it felt great, but that the best thing for me was thinking that Rankin *wanted* to do those things with me. It wasn't the sex, really. I mean, you can kind of do that on your own, right? But having this other person want to do it with you, that's pretty special. It means he

255

likes you. At least, it should.

I keep wondering what Rankin was thinking when he did those things with me. Had someone done those things to him? Is he really gay? Did he like me at all? I guess I won't ever be able to answer those questions. I asked the doc, and he said that when people hurt us, the best thing to do isn't to ask why they did it but to remind ourselves that it wasn't our fault.

In other words, either he doesn't know what Rankin's deal is or won't tell me.

Either way, I'm not sure I believe him. Maybe it *was* partly my fault. It's not like I made Rankin stop. It's not like I didn't *like* what we did. It's not like I didn't want to do it. At least some part of me wanted to.

To change the subject, I asked if Martha was going to be okay. Martha hasn't said anything since that night—not even "frex"—and I worry that she's totally regressing, which is a term I learned from Cat Poop. Basically, it means that whatever good has happened to her might have been erased by what happened with Sadie. I love how shrinks have a special word for everything that can be wrong with you.

Cat Poop said he didn't know. But there was something in his voice that made me think he didn't believe she would be all right. I wanted to ask him more about it, because I figured it had something to do with why she's here in the first place. But I knew he wouldn't tell me anything, so I just said I hoped she would be okay.

I found out later, though. I asked Frank. Like I said, Frank can be kind of a jerk. But he likes to think he knows a lot, so when I saw him later on, I started talking about how awful what happened to Sadie was. "Martha was really upset about it," I said, knowing he would want to tell me everything he knew about it.

"Yeah, well, who can blame her?" said Frank. "She probably thought it was happening again."

"Thought what was happening?" I said.

He laughed again. "Oh, right. They don't let you listen to the news in here. Kid's dad shot her mother."

"Martha's dad?" I said.

"Blew her open with a shotgun," said Frank. "Then killed himself. The kid saw the whole thing. When they found her, she was sitting between them on the kitchen floor, holding that damn stuffed rabbit. She'd been there two or three days. Aunt or something went over after she kept calling and getting no answer."

"You're kidding," I said.

"It was all over the papers," said Frank. "I forgot, they only let you look at the funny papers." He laughed. "Funny papers—get it?"

I ignored him and walked away. All I could think about was Martha sitting in that kitchen. No wonder she flipped when she saw Sadie. Poor kid. And I thought I had problems. If we're keeping score, I think Martha just pulled way ahead of the rest of us.

Day 39

I was sitting in Cat Poop's office today and all of a sudden I asked him, "How do I know if I'm really gay or not?" It just popped out of my mouth, but once it was out there I really wanted to know.

Cat Poop leaned back in his chair and looked at me. "What's your favorite color?"

I told him it was blue. Then he asked me why.

"Why what?" I asked back.

"Why is blue your favorite color?" he said.

It seems like a dumb question, right? I mean, why do you like anything? I told him I like blue because when I look at blue things, they usually make me feel good.

"Okay," he said. "Now what's your favorite song?"

I told him it was Lolly Dreambox's "Snow Cold Sunday." At least right now. I'm sure next week it will be something else. That's how it is when you're fifteen.

He asked me again why it was my favorite. I said because whenever I hear it I want to sing along. I picture myself on a stage, singing, and it makes me feel good.

"Okay," he said. "What do your favorite color and your favorite song have in common?"

The answer is that they both make me feel good, although in different ways. That wasn't too hard to figure out. But then he said, "How do you feel when you think about girls?"

That seemed like a trick question to me. There are a lot of different ways to answer it. So I asked him to be more specific, and he asked how I felt about girls when I thought about going out with them, like as a boyfriend.

I said I didn't really feel any particular way about it. It didn't make me feel good or bad. "Sort of like vanilla ice cream," I said.

Then he asked me the same thing about guys. I got kind of embarrassed, because I've never talked with anyone about how guys make me feel. But finally I said that when I think about going out with a guy, it makes me feel all kinds of things. I feel excited and scared at the same time.

"Sometimes we don't know why we like certain things," Cat Poop said. "Or at least we can't put into words why we like them. We just know that we do. Being gay or straight—or something in between—is often like that. We just like one thing or another because of how it makes us feel."

That still didn't answer my question, and I said so. I asked him how I would know for sure that I'm gay. "Maybe it's just something I feel right now," I said.

He said that maybe it was, which didn't make me feel any better. "The only thing you can do is listen to your feelings," he said. "If you're honest about what you feel, you'll know what's true about yourself."

I swear, sometimes he's like one of those weird old guys in martial arts movies who show up and say all kinds of crazy crap that the hero has to figure out so he can find the sword or save the girl or kick the bad guy's ass. You know, like, "Find the whistling pine tree and ask it for the key," or something.

I guess I know what he means, though. It was like the night I was with Sadie, when I knew I couldn't have sex with her. It just didn't feel right. Yeah, maybe it would feel different with another girl, but I don't think so. With Rankin I *knew*. Even though he wasn't the right guy, being with a guy felt right to me. Everything about what we did was scary and weird, but I knew it was what I wanted. Not with Rankin, and definitely not here, but someday with someone else. Someone I like.

Then Cat Poop brought up the idea of telling my parents. I said I wasn't sure if I could do that or not.

"So you've never talked about it with them?" he asked.

"We don't talk in my family," I said. "We assume."

"What do you mean by that?" he said.

"I mean my parents assume," I explained. "They assume that Amanda and I will ask them if we have questions about anything. Otherwise, they assume it's all good with us."

"And do you ever talk to them?"

I gave him a look. "You've met them," I said. "What do you think?"

Now that I'm thinking about it, I don't think my parents have any gay friends, at least none that I know of. So I don't really know how they feel about the whole gay thing. Besides, I think it's different when it's your kid you're talking about and not some stranger. I know my mother is all into the idea of having grandkids someday, and my dad teases us about how he's going to screen everyone Amanda and I bring home when we start dating. I can't exactly see him sitting my date down and asking him what his favorite football team is.

I asked Cat Poop if he would tell my parents if he was me, and of course he said he couldn't make that decision for me. I figured he would say that, but it was worth a shot. So then I asked him if he had any advice on how to decide whether or not to do it.

"You could practice telling them," he suggested.

"You mean walk through it in my head?" I said.

"No, I mean with me," said Cat Poop.

"You don't look much like my mom," I informed him. "Even without the goatee."

He smiled. "I could play your dad, then," he said.

"I don't know," I told him. "That's kind of weird."

"Well, think about it," he said.

So now I'm thinking about it. I'm imagining sitting down with my parents and actually saying, "I'm gay." And you know what? It makes me a little mad. I mean, straight guys don't have to sit their parents down and tell them they like girls. Everyone just assumes that they do. But if you're gay, everybody makes this ginormous deal out of it. You practically have to hold a news conference and take out an ad in the newspaper. Why? Just because it's not what most people do? That doesn't seem fair.

Why *should* my parents know? So they can get used to the idea of not having a daughter-in-law? So they can practice imagining me walking down the aisle with a guy? I don't get it. Why is it that you have to *warn* people about who you are? Why can't it just be something that happens?

I know why. I'm just blowing off steam. It's a lot of pressure, telling someone something like that. It's like you're committing to it. "Mom, dad, I've thought about it a lot, and I've decided I'm gay." Like you've read all the brochures and comparison shopped. Or finally decided what college to go to. Only if you're wrong, you can't exactly get a refund or switch schools. Well, I guess you could, but then you've gotten every-one all excited for nothing.

DAY 40

Funny, Rankin has been gone for almost a week, and nobody has asked where he is or what happened to him. I asked Cat Poop about him today, but all he would say was that Rankin had been transferred somewhere else. Like he got a new job or something.

He also read me Sadie's suicide note. I didn't even know she'd left a note. Cat Poop said he'd waited for some time to go by before telling me so that I wouldn't be as upset about it. I told him that was big of him.

So he read it to me. It was his voice talking, but what I heard was Sadie.

"Hey, everyone," she said. "I guess by now you know I won't be around anymore. Maybe some of you will miss me, and maybe some of you won't. I'll miss you guys. It's been fun. But it's time to go. No one can save me this time. Not even Sam. I'll see you all on the other side, I guess. Love, Sadie."

That was it. Nothing about why. Nothing about what was going on in her head. Nothing about . . . me.

"What the hell kind of note is that?" I said. "She didn't say anything. It's just stupid."

Then I got mad. Really mad. "Who does she think she is?" I asked Cat Poop. "She goes and kills herself and all she has to say about it is 'see you on the other side'? That's completely fucked up."

"Maybe it's all she could say," said Cat Poop. "Maybe she didn't really know why she was doing it."

"How can you not know?" I said.

"Why do you think she did it?" he said, pulling the old answering-a-question-with-a-question bullshit.

The thing is, I didn't know. But I was afraid I did. I was afraid it was because I couldn't sleep with her. I was afraid it was because she felt rejected, the way I did with Burke. And with Allie. If that was true, then I knew why she wanted to kill herself. I knew exactly why.

"What are you thinking?" Cat Poop asked me.

I couldn't say it. I just couldn't. If I said it, I knew

it would be true. But as long as I kept it inside, as long as it was a secret, it couldn't be.

"You're afraid it was because of you?"

Goddamn it, I don't know how he does that, but the doc always manages to ask you the one question you really don't want him to.

I nodded, but I still didn't say it. I didn't let it out. Finally, when I couldn't stand it anymore, I said, "Do you?"

When he shook his head, I almost threw up. "No," he said. "I don't."

"Then why the fuck did you ask me?" I practically yelled. I only say "fuck" when I'm really pissed off. Otherwise, I think it kind of ruins the effect. But right then I *was* really pissed off. Fucking pissed off.

"Because I had a feeling you might be thinking that," he said.

I glared at him. "You're a real asshole," I said. "You know that?"

He ignored me. "There's something else," he said. "She wrote a poem."

"A poem?" I said. That was totally not a Sadie thing to do.

Cat Poop handed me the letter. Down at the bottom, after the note, Sadie had written:

Seven little crazy kids chopping up sticks;
One burnt her daddy up and then there were six.
Six little crazy kids playing with a hive;
One tattooed himself to death and then there
were five.
Five little crazy kids on a cellar door;
One went all schizo and then there were four.
Four little crazy kids going out to sea;
One wouldn't say a word, and then there were
three.
Three little crazy kids walking to the zoo;
One jerked himself too much and then there were
two.
Two little crazy kids sitting in the sun;
One took a bunch of pills and then there was one.
One little crazy kid left all alone;
He went and slit his wrists, and then there were
none.

"So this is what we were to her," I said. "Just a list of problems."

"I don't think that's it," said Cat Poop. "I think she wanted to believe that you all had something in common."

"Being crazy?" I said.

He nodded. "It probably made her feel better about herself."

Maybe so, but it doesn't make me feel any better. In fact, I'm even madder at her than I was before. I'm mad because she turned out to be such a phony. She wanted me—and everyone else—to think she was so cool and nothing could bother her. She wanted us to believe that she really had it all together. And we did. Or at least I did.

But she wasn't together. She wasn't cool and strong and smarter than everyone else. She was afraid. She was afraid we'd all see the real her one day and that we wouldn't like it. Well, I *don't* like it. I don't like that she lied to me and made me think she was someone she wasn't. I don't like that she pretended to be cool with everything but was really running away. I don't like that I want to be sad about her dying but I can't because I'm too mad at her.

First Allie and now Sadie. They both left me. And even though Sadie never said it, part of me still wonders if it's because I'm gay. Allie couldn't handle it. Maybe Sadie couldn't either.

So now it's just me, Juliet, and Martha. The last three little soldier boys. I guess everyone waiting behind the velvet ropes to get in decided to go to a different club or something. Tonight after dinner, me and Juliet were sitting in the lounge. I don't know why, but I asked her, "Did you like Sadie?"

Juliet put down the book she was reading. "I liked her the way you like a hurt dog," she said.

"What do you mean?" I asked her.

"You feel sorry for it, and you want to help it, but you're not sure it won't bite you when you're not looking," Juliet said.

Now I know Juliet says some weird stuff. But sometimes she gets it exactly right, like occasionally her craziness goes away long enough for her to really see you. I knew what she meant. Sadie was kind of like that. She was always wagging her tail and making you think she liked you, but I'm not sure she really liked any of us any more than she liked herself.

"What about Rankin?" I asked Juliet.

She shook her head. "I never liked him," she said. "Did you?"

As far as I know, she doesn't know anything about what happened with Rankin and me. I think only Moonie, Goody, and Carl know, and I don't think they would say anything. I guess they've seen so many crazy things that they forget about them pretty fast or at least get really good at pretending to.

I shrugged. "I thought we were friends," I told her. "But I guess I didn't like him. Not really."

"Why would you be friends with someone you didn't like?" Juliet asked me. For a second she reminded me of Cat Poop, and I pictured her with a pad and pencil.

"Sometimes you don't know you don't like someone until you've been around them for a while," I said.

"I do," said Juliet. "I can always tell if I like someone or not."

I asked her how.

"I get itchy when I'm near them," she said. "I think I'm allergic to dangerous people. Rankin made me itch."

You might think she's just nuts, but it makes as much sense as anything else. I mean, how *do* you know if people are good for you or not? It's not like they come with an FDA APPROVED sticker or anything.

That made me think about Allie again and whether or not we're still friends. It's not like this was our first fight. It was just a lot more serious than other fights we've had. What if she calls and apologizes for dumping me? Would I forgive her?

Man, that's a hard one. It's not like we just had a

fight over what movie to go to. She cut me out because Burke told her I kissed him. She didn't even stop to ask me if it was true.

But it *was* true. That's the thing. If she'd asked me then, I would have said Burke was lying or that I was joking around with him. I would never have told her that I was gay, because I couldn't even tell myself that I was. So she was kind of right. Not to break our friendship up the way she did but about being angry. I don't even know if she was angrier about me maybe being gay or me kissing her boyfriend. She never gave me the chance to ask.

I know Allie pretty well, and I don't think she'd stop being my friend because I'm gay. If I had just told her, things might have been different. Now I don't know if I'll ever get the chance.

Day 41

"I'm pretty sure I'm gay, and I'd like to find out more about what that means."

My dad was really quiet for a while. Then he said, "You're too young to know something like that."

Only it wasn't my dad. It was Cat Poop. Today I had my dress rehearsal with him. My dress rehearsal for telling my parents about myself. I decided last night that I would do it. I mean, if I'm going to go to all the trouble of being gay and everything, I might as well tell people.

Cat Poop offered to be both my dad and my mom, but the idea of my mom needing to shave really didn't work for me, so I told him we could stick to my dad.

Besides, I think my father will be the hard one to deal with, anyway. Dads usually are.

So he sits in the chair across from me and I try to start. Only I can't think of anything that doesn't sound dumb. "I have something to tell you" just sounds like bad soap opera dialogue. "There's something you need to know about me" is even worse, like you're about to announce that you have leukemia or are a secret agent or something. Really, everything sounds way too dramatic.

I finally said, "I want to talk to you about why I hurt myself." Then I explained about Allie and Burke and how I was afraid of the feelings I had for Burke and about how Allie had stopped being my friend because of it.

That's when my "dad" said the thing about me being too young to know what I want. I was a little shocked at how hostile he sounded. Then I remembered that Cat Poop was playing a part. He didn't know how my father would really respond, so he was trying one possible way to see what I did.

"I know I'm young," I said. "But I also know how strong these feelings are, and I think I need to see what they mean." It didn't sound like me at all, but it was true. Besides, parents like it when you talk like that. It makes you sound more like them. Although now that I think about it, maybe that will just scare them more.

"You just need to see a shrink," said Cat Poop Dad. "That will fix you."

I wanted to laugh, but the doc looked really serious. I tried to imagine my dad really saying that. I don't think he ever would, but it scared me to think that he *could*. I said, "I *have* been seeing a shrink, and he's helped me understand a lot of things about myself. I'd like to keep talking to him if it's okay with you, but I don't think I need to be fixed. I just need to talk about some stuff."

"What am I going to tell your grandmother?" asked Cat Poop. "What am I supposed to tell people?"

I took a deep breath and faced him. "Tell them the truth," I said. "I'm not ashamed of myself. If you are, I'm sorry. But I don't think there's anything for you to be ashamed of."

Cat Poop nodded. "Not bad," he said. "Shall we try a different reaction?"

We went through some more scenes, or whatever you'd call them. Sometimes my dad was okay with what I had to say, and other times he was angry. By the time we were done I was exhausted. I don't know how movie stars do the same scene over and over like that. It takes a lot out of you.

Cat Poop asked me how the different reactions made me feel. I told him that, obviously, the ones where my dad wasn't upset were the best. Then he asked me which one I thought was most likely to happen.

I wish I knew. I really do. But I don't. You'd think that after living with these people for fifteen years I'd know a little something about them. But right now I feel like I don't know my parents at all. I guess when you get down to it, I've never really thought about them as *people*. They've always been my parents. Now I have to think about them as people with feelings. What a pain.

The funny thing is, I bet they feel the same way. I bet they sit around at home wondering how to talk to this kid who looks like their son but acts like someone they've never met in their lives. In a way, that makes me feel a little bit better. It's like we're all going to find out who we are. But it's still scary. I'm still worried that there's a tiny, tiny chance that they'll completely flip out and disown me.

We'll find out on Sunday.

Day 42

Someone new arrived today, so apparently our nuthouse is still the hottest club in town after all. He says
his name is Squirrel. I can't imagine anyone would
name a kid that, but it's what he wants to be called.
And it sort of fits him. He's really skinny, and he darts
his eyes all over the place when he's talking, like he's
afraid that if he looks right at you, you'll explode.

We met him in group today. As the rest of us introduced ourselves, I couldn't help thinking about my
first day. Did I look as freaked out as Squirrel did?
Probably. Then again, I had Bone, Alice, and Sadie in
my group. That would freak anyone out. Squirrel just
has me, Juliet, and Martha. I don't think any of us are

all that scary. Well, maybe Juliet is, but only once you get to know her. Even then, she's not so bad.

I don't know what Squirrel's problem is. He didn't say. But if I had to take a guess, I'd say he's probably got a couple of things going on. Maybe drugs. Maybe depression. Maybe both. You kind of start to catch on to this stuff when you've been here a while. It's almost like every problem has a different smell. Squirrel smells like a combination of cigarette ashes and cotton candy. It's not pretty.

I wonder if everyone knew right off that I'd tried to kill myself. I mean, I did have bandages on my wrists, so it wasn't like it was a total mystery. They didn't know about the gay thing, though. They couldn't see that.

Except maybe Rankin. Maybe he knew. Why else would he have done what he did? Sure, I was the only other guy here. But would he have done that with Bone? *Did* he do that with Bone? I think he probably would have if he'd had the chance. It's not like he was in love with me or anything. It was just something he did. I didn't mean anything to him. Then again, he didn't really mean anything to me either, so I guess that makes us even.

Funny, I've fooled around with a guy I didn't care

about, and the one guy I *have* cared about would never even think about touching me. Sometimes I wonder if Burke does ever think about me. I mean, he and Allie must have talked about what happened. I wonder if he ever imagines what it would be like if we did do anything. I mean, I've wondered about what it would be like with Allie even though she's a girl. And since Burke knows I like him, wouldn't he *have* to think about it? Or is the idea of it so disgusting that he can't even imagine it?

I wonder if Allie thinks about what it would be like to have sex with me. That's a little harder to imagine. But I know Allie. She dwells on stuff. Forever. "Letting go" is a foreign concept to her. Three years ago, Meg Crenshaw made a comment about how a sweater Allie wore made her look like a Sunday School teacher. Allie *still* hasn't forgotten it.

I honestly don't know what I'm going to do about that. Not about the sweater. About how Allie feels. Not that it's totally up to me. Allie has a say in it, too. So does Burke, I guess. It sounds weird, but I really don't think I care what he thinks of me anymore. Allie is more important to me than he is. But am I more important to her than Burke? I guess I wouldn't blame her if she picked her boyfriend over me. I'd be really pissed off, though.

Anyway, back to Squirrel. I talked to him a little bit this afternoon. He's still on the Wonder Drug, so I don't think it's quite sunk in yet that he's in a psych ward. Part of me wanted to tell him. Then I remembered how cool it was to fly around in space smelling clean air, and I decided not to.

Instead, we played Monopoly. I know, it's the most boring game in existence. But it's good for killing time, and you don't have to think too much about it. Juliet and Martha played, too. Juliet was the top hat, Martha was the little dog, I was the shoe, and Squirrel was the race car.

Martha won. She bought up all the red properties and set up hotels there, and that wiped the rest of us out. For someone who barely says anything, that girl is one tough landlord. When I couldn't pay the rent on Indiana Avenue, she made me give her Marvin Gardens *and* the Reading Railroad. She's like a little Donald Trump, only with better hair.

Afterward, the four of us sat there watching the snow fall outside. For some reason, I counted, and I realized that I'm getting out of here on Valentine's Day. That's kind of ironic, don't you think? I mean, I ended up here because I was all heartbroken over

Burke. Now I'm getting out on the most romantic day of the year.

Maybe I should make Burke a valentine. Just kidding. I'm so over him. Sure, he's cute. And nice. And funny. Okay, so maybe I'm not *totally* over him. But there's that whole being straight thing. That's kind of a problem as far as he and I being boyfriends go.

Besides, I don't think it was really him I wanted. It was the idea of him. I saw how happy he made Allie. *Makes* Allie. Present tense. At least, I assume they're still together.

Maybe someday I'll have a boyfriend to give a valentine to. Thinking about that kind of makes me sick, actually. I'm not exactly romantic, you know? And did you know that Valentine's Day originally started when this emperor like a million years ago made marriage illegal because he thought it made soldiers weak? This priest—Valentine—married people in secret anyway, and he ended up having his head cut off because of it. So the first Valentine was some guy's head. There's some history for you.

It's sort of perfect, when you think about it. Isn't falling in love a lot like losing your head?

Day 43

If you ever have to tell your parents you're gay, there's only one thing I can promise you: However you think they'll react, they won't.

I tried not to think about it too much, but I was awake almost all night doing exactly that. I kept running through the different scenarios that I'd rehearsed the other day with Cat Poop.

What actually happened wasn't like anything we did, though. Well, it was and it wasn't. It was more like a little bit of everything we did.

Things started off kind of badly because my parents were late. I don't know why, but they were arguing about it when they got here. Something about my mother not being ready on time or my father having to stop for gas. It doesn't matter. It's just that they were already in a weird mood. Oh, and they brought Amanda with them, which was actually kind of good, because I wanted her to hear what I had to say, too.

So my parents were kind of bickering, not really fighting but being snappy with each other. Amanda was sitting there rolling her eyes the way she does when she's completely embarrassed for people to know that she's related to our mom and dad. And I was trying not to throw up.

Cat Poop started things off by reminding my parents that I would be coming home soon. As in two days. That snapped them out of their moods a little bit. My mother got all smiley and my father kept nodding, like someone had asked him a question and he was answering yes. Amanda hunched down in her seat, chewed on the ends of her hair, and tried to disappear. I think she's about at the end of her patience with my parents. It's good that I'm coming home to distract them.

Then Cat Poop started talking about how well I've been doing in the hospital and how much progress we've made. It was all doctor crap, and I knew he was saying it to make me look healthy and not crazy before

I dropped the big bomb on everyone. I was glad he did it, because my parents are really into what doctors have to say about stuff. One could tell them their heads were made out of blue cheese and they'd probably buy it.

Once we'd established the fact that I wasn't going to go all *Amityville Horror* on them and kill them in their sleep when I got home, Cat Poop asked me if there was anything I wanted to tell them. That was my cue to spill the news. Only I couldn't even remember my name right then. It was like everything had gone blank inside my head. I turned into my dad and just started nodding, like I was agreeing with something he had said. I was like this giant bobble-head doll sitting there in the chair nodding, nodding, nodding.

Because I wasn't saying anything, my mother started talking. She talked about the new curtains she'd put up in my room, and about how much the dog missed me, and how my grandmother was making cookies—chocolate chip cookies—and was going to bring them over when I came home. I sat there and watched her mouth open and close, wondering how she could talk so fast and still breathe.

Then my father started talking, too, saying stuff to my mother like, "Marjorie, Jeff doesn't care about the curtains" and, to me, "How'd you like to go skiing next weekend?"

They were both talking at once. Cat Poop was trying to interrupt them, but they were ignoring him. The only one *not* talking besides me was Amanda, so I looked at her and said, "How would you like to have a gay brother?"

Then everyone stopped talking and stared at me. Amanda stopped chewing her hair and sat up. "That would be okay with me," she said. "Why?"

"Because you do," I told her.

My mother gave a little gasp. Amanda sat there with her mouth open. My father said, "Sweet Jesus Christ on a biscuit." I swear to God that's what he said. *Sweet Jesus Christ on a biscuit.*

"You're *gay*?" Amanda said, really emphasizing the gay part so that it sounded like the longest word anyone had every said. "As in *gay*?"

"Yeah," I said. "I'm pretty sure I am."

My father said the thing about Jesus on a biscuit again and my mother said, "Eric," like he was five years old. Then she shook her head and said, "I don't understand. What do you mean you're gay?"

I thought for a second I was going to have to explain to her what gay meant. Then I realized she thought I was joking, or confused, or maybe both. I guess she thought maybe *I* didn't know what gay meant.

"I'm gay," I said, not sure how else to say it.

"You're fifteen," she said. "You can't be gay."

"Sure he can," Amanda said. She sounded all excited, like this was her big chance to show off something she knew that my mother didn't. "My friend Katrina from dance class's brother is gay and he's fifteen." She looked at me. "Hey, maybe I can set you guys up. Evan is really cute."

"Jeff," my mother said, using the tone she gets when she's about to explain something to you, "you're too young to know if you're gay or not."

"Do you care if I am?" I asked her.

"Of course I care," she said. "I mean, I don't *care*, but I care about you, and if you *were* gay, then I'd be okay with it."

"Well, I am," I said. "So I hope you're really okay with it and not just saying that."

My father still hadn't said anything. He had this look on his face like he was trying to figure out a joke someone had told him and that he knew should be funny but didn't understand why.

"Dad?" I said. "Are you all right?"

"What?" he said. Then he shook his head, like he was trying to clear it. "So, this gay thing," he said. "Is that why you, well, you know." He waved his hands in the air, like he couldn't think of the words he needed.

I shook my head. "Not really," I said. "It's part of it, but it's not everything."

"I think we have a lot to talk about," Cat Poop said, saving me. "I know you all probably have questions for Jeff, and I know there are things he wants to tell you. So let's just start at the beginning and go from there."

And that's what we did. For about four hours. I can't even remember everything we talked about. There was some yelling, a little crying, and finally a big family hug, which is a miracle all on its own. By the time my parents left, I think they were starting to understand that this isn't just some phase I'm going through or something I'm doing to get back at them. They don't get it all yet. Then again, neither do I.

Day 44

I had a dream about Sadie last night. She and I were walking on a beach, talking about whatever we wanted and having a good time. Then, all of a sudden, she ran into the ocean. I thought she was playing, so I followed her. She was laughing and kept looking back to see if I was behind her.

She started swimming, and I swam after her. She swam way out, and I was afraid we were going too far. I kept calling for her to slow down, but she wouldn't.

I couldn't keep up with her, so I stopped swimming and let her get ahead. Finally she stopped and turned around. She called for me to come out to where she was, and I did. When I got there, she said, "Catch me if you can!" and dived down.

I watched her swim beneath me. The water was clear, and I could see her kicking her legs hard and going deeper and deeper, down to where the water turned dark blue. Her hair was floating out around her head, and silver bubbles were coming from her mouth. I took a deep breath and dived after her, trying to catch her.

She turned in the water and waved at me, trying to get me to come deeper. My chest was starting to burn because I was running out of air, and I pointed to the surface to tell her we should go up. She shook her head, and I saw her laugh underwater. Millions of bubbles shot out of her mouth and surrounded me like a net. I couldn't see. Then I felt a hand grab my foot and pull me down.

I tried to swim up, but that hand was strong. It was Sadie's hand. Through the bubbles I saw her dragging me into the dark water. She was laughing and laughing. I realized that she wanted to keep going, and she wanted to take me with her.

I kicked as hard as I could, trying to get her hand off my foot. I just kicked and kicked while I clawed at the water. Finally I got free and started to shoot toward the surface. I could see the light shining down, and I reached for it.

I looked down once more and saw Sadie looking up at me. Her face got smaller and smaller as I flew up through the water. She wasn't smiling anymore. She was just watching me. Watching me leave her under the water.

I woke up when my head broke through the waves. I was gasping, and my chest felt like it was on fire. I looked all around my room, almost expecting to see that I was on a beach and soaking wet.

I don't know what the dream means. I don't know why Sadie wanted to try to drown me. I don't know why she laughed at me like she did. I'm just glad I got away from her.

Day 45

One of the best T-shirts I ever saw said, I WAS HAPPY ONCE, BUT I'M BETTER NOW.

I'm going home today. Most people would say that they were "happy" about that. And I guess I am. I mean I am.

I said good-bye to Martha and Juliet. Martha's staying. For a few more weeks, anyway. Then she's going to live with her aunt. She still isn't saying much. I think they're keeping her on the Wonder Drug. Poor kid. She definitely got a bad deal.

Juliet is leaving next week. It turns out her parents are super religious. Juliet told me they think she's possessed by demons. Seriously. They believe in that kind of stuff. They want her to let the people at their church do some kind of healing ritual for her. She says she's thinking about it. It's weird, but I used to think she was the craziest one in here. Now she seems kind of normal. I don't know if she's gotten less crazy or I've gotten more crazy. Probably it's a little of both.

Oh, yeah, then there's Squirrel. I still don't get him. Juliet said she'll find out what his story is and let me know. She won't, though. She'll forget about me as soon as she's out of here. Maybe even as soon as I walk out the door. She doesn't want to remember, and I can't blame her. She'll probably convince herself we were all ghosts, or a dream.

I wonder how many of us there are all over the world, how many kids in how many hospitals. How many Alices and Bones and Juliets and Rankins. How many Sadies and Marthas and Squirrels. How many Jeffs. And I wonder how many of us get out. I wonder how many of us are "happy."

I had my last session with Cat Poop—I mean, Dr. Katzrupus—this morning. Only it turns out it wasn't my last one. I'll be seeing him once a week. At least for a while. I'm okay with that.

He said that I have to remember that even though I've changed a lot in here, I'm going back to a world that hasn't changed. That's going to be the hardest part, I think, seeing all the people who were in my life before. They don't know what's happened to me. They're going to expect to have the same old Jeff back. But I'm not the same old Jeff. I hope they're ready for that. I hope *I'm* ready for that.

I'm still kind of a mess. But I think we all are. No one's got it all together. I don't think you ever do get it totally together. Probably if you did manage to do it you'd spontaneously combust. I think that's a law of nature. If you ever manage to become perfect, you have to die instantly before you ruin things for everyone else.

It kind of feels like the last night of summer camp. For a couple of years I went to this place called Camp Mikigwani. For the two weeks I was there I hated everything about it, the swimming, the campfire sing-alongs, the stupid crafts, the other kids. Everything. Then, the night before my parents came to pick me up, I'd start to wish I could stay for another two weeks. One summer I even asked my parents if I could. They said yes, and for about three seconds I was really happy. But as soon as they drove away, I started hating the place again and was miserable for another two weeks.

Part of me wants to stay here where people sort of understand me. But I know I have to leave. My vacation is over, and it's time to let some new campers in.

I haven't decided what to do about the Allie thing yet. Maybe I'll call her. Or maybe I'll send her here to talk to Dr. Katzrupus for forty-five days. I don't think she'd hold out as long as I did. I bet he'd break her in two weeks. She can't keep a secret.

Not that there are any secrets to keep anymore. I think I've told all of mine. Well, most of them. The big ones. You've got to keep some stuff to yourself, otherwise there's no reason for people to get to know you.

I almost forgot. It's Valentine's Day. Allie and I always used to give each other silly valentines, mostly to make us feel better about not having *real* valentines to give them to. But also because we really do care about each other. Did care? Do care? I don't know.

This will be the first year we haven't done it. But what if I *was* going to give her a valentine? What would it say? Maybe something like this:

I'M SORRY I COULDN'T TALK TO YOU. I'M SORRY
I HURT YOU. I DIDN'T MEAN TO. YOU'RE MY
BEST FRIEND, AND I WANT YOU BACK. I KNOW

I'M SORT OF A DIFFERENT PERSON NOW, BUT I
HOPE YOU'LL GIVE ME A CHANCE. I HAVE A LOT
TO TELL YOU.

LOVE,
JEFF

I could never send that. It's too sappy. Even worse
than hugging. Still, Allie kind of falls for that sort of
thing. Maybe it would work. Or maybe she would just
tear it up. I really don't know anymore.

I wonder if my parents would think it was weird if
I asked them to stop at the card store on the way
home.

1-866-4-U-TREVOR
1-866-488-7386

Website: www.thetrevorproject.org
MySpace: www.myspace.com/trevorproject

THE NATIONAL SUICIDE PREVENTION LIFELINE

The National Suicide Prevention Lifeline is a 24-hour, toll-free service providing information and referrals to people struggling with thoughts of self-harm. Their counselors can connect you with support organizations in your area that offer immediate help.

1-800-273-TALK
1-800-273-8255

Website: www.suicidepreventionlifeline.org
MySpace: www.myspace.com/suicidepreventionlifeline

If you are depressed or having thoughts about suicide you are not alone. Many of us have these thoughts, and it does not mean you're a freak or crazy or a bad person. There are numerous causes of depression and suicidal thoughts, and it's important that you talk to someone about how you're feeling. Trust me—no matter how horrible you feel or how bad things seem, there is always a way out. Suicide is never your only option.

If you feel safe talking to a friend or a parent or someone else you trust, ask them to help you find someone qualified to work with you to understand your feelings and to provide the support you need. If you do not feel you can speak to anyone you know about your feelings, there are online and telephone services available providing confidential assistance to people struggling with thoughts of suicide. Two of the most respected are:

THE TREVOR PROJECT

The Trevor Project is a 24-hour, toll-free service that provides help for gay, lesbian, bisexual, transgender, and questioning young people in crisis. If you are gay or think you might be gay, and would like to speak to someone about your thoughts of depression or suicide, call the number on the next page to reach a counselor. You can also visit the group's website or MySpace page for more information.